About

The summer she turned thirteen, ——— left the children's section of the library and entered an aisle full of Mills & Boon® novels. She promptly pulled out a book, sat on the floor, and read the entire story. It has been a love affair that has lasted for over thirty years.

Despite a fantastic job working part-time as a physician in the Alaskan Bush (think *Northern Exposure* and *ER*, minus the beautiful mountains and George Clooney), she also enjoys being at home in the gorgeous Black Hills of South Dakota, riding her dirt bike with her three wonderful kids and beyond patient husband. But, whether at home or at work, every morning is spent creating the stories she loves so much. Her motto? Life is too short to do anything less than what you absolutely love. She counts herself lucky to have two jobs she adores, and incredibly blessed to be a part of Mills & Boon's family of talented authors.

Praise for Aimee Carson

'Oh, my, what a fantastic debut by Aimee Carson. I loved it! It really has everything that I like in a good contemporary romance: a feisty heroine who is far from perfect, snappy dialogue and sizzling chemistry—and I mean sizzling. *That* scene in the elevator…phew! The romance and relationship between Alyssa and Paulo is actually quite simple, but perfectly done. Aimee's writing flows beautifully, and she has created two great characters. I applaud her for Alyssa's 'bad girl' roots, I loved her! The book is well written and developed, with plenty of sass and sparkle. I can't wait to read more from Aimee in the future.'
—www.everyday-is-the-same.blogspot.com on
Secret History of a Good Girl

The Best Mistake of Her Life

Aimee Carson

MILLS & BOON

All the characters in this book have no existence outside the imagination of the author, and have no relation whatsoever to anyone bearing the same name or names. They are not even distantly inspired by any individual known or unknown to the author, and all the incidents are pure invention.

All Rights Reserved including the right of reproduction in whole or in part in any form. This edition is published by arrangement with Harlequin Enterprises II B.V./S.à.r.l. The text of this publication or any part thereof may not be reproduced or transmitted in any form or by any means, electronic or mechanical, including photocopying, recording, storage in an information retrieval system, or otherwise, without the written permission of the publisher.

This book is sold subject to the condition that it shall not, by way of trade or otherwise, be lent, resold, hired out or otherwise circulated without the prior consent of the publisher in any form of binding or cover other than that in which it is published and without a similar condition including this condition being imposed on the subsequent purchaser.

® and ™ are trademarks owned and used by the trademark owner and/or its licensee. Trademarks marked with ® are registered with the United Kingdom Patent Office and/or the Office for Harmonisation in the Internal Market and in other countries.

First published in Great Britain 2012
by Mills & Boon, an imprint of Harlequin (UK) Limited,
Eton House, 18-24 Paradise Road, Richmond, Surrey TW9 1SR

© Aimee Carson 2012

ISBN: 978 0 263 90276 1
ebook ISBN: 978 1 408 99772 7

06-1012

Harlequin (UK) policy is to use papers that are natural, renewable and recyclable products and made from wood grown in sustainable forests. The logging and manufacturing processes conform to the legal environmental regulations of the country of origin.

Printed and bound in Spain
by Blackprint CPI, Barcelona

Also by Aimee Carson

Dare She Kiss & Tell?
How to Win the Dating War
Secret History of a Good Girl*

*Published as part of the *Mills & Boon Loves...* anthology.

**Did you know these are also available as eBooks?
Visit www.millsandboon.co.uk**

CHAPTER ONE

MEMPHIS James stood on the twenty-second floor of the downtown Miami building and looked down at the camera crew on the street below, spectators lining the barricade like curious ants. There was only one chance to get the high-fall right—no do-overs possible. Along with the stunt engineer, Memphis had meticulously checked and rechecked every detail, including his harness, the cable hoist and the wind conditions. No matter how crazy the stunt, death wasn't likely—more of a distant possibility that hinged on either mechanical error or miscalculation, so nothing was left to chance. Memphis *never* left anything to chance.

It was a necessary compulsion in this twisted business of mocking gravity. Because if his focus was off, mistakes were made and he could be killed or, at the very least, sustain a dream-crushing injury.

Or worse...someone else might pay the price.

For one second the memory resurfaced, just like it always did before a high-fall. In a now-familiar sequence of reactions, Memphis's chest cinched tight, his stomach balled into a knot and his heart beat mercilessly against his ribs.

Willing his muscles to relax, Memphis forced the memory from his mind as he gazed down at the two-hundred-plus feet between him and the empty pavement. There was nothing to break his fall save the camera on the ground that would record his descent. His lips twisted wryly. He liked the idea that if something went wrong—and he hit the pavement traveling approximately eighty miles per hour—his last seconds on earth would be recorded for posterity.

If he was checking out, he'd do it with flair and with his name on everyone's lips.

The stunt engineer broke into his thoughts. "Everything's set. Wind speed steady at five mph."

With one last look at the ground below, Memphis said, "That's as good as we'll get."

"You ready?"

Now rock-steady, his pulse at a regular rate, Memphis took his position in front of the temporary window constructed of safety glass. "I'm always ready." A grin slipped up his face. "But gravity is a bitch of a mistress."

"An unforgiving one, to be sure," the man returned with a chuckle.

Memphis's grin grew bigger in anticipation. "So let's not keep her waiting."

One hand clutching the barricade, Kate Anderson shaded her eyes from the sun and stared up at the tiny hub of activity twenty-two stories above the ground. A gentle breeze carried a hint of the salty Atlantic Ocean tinged with hot pavement, and the crowd of curious gawkers pressed in around her, making the warm Miami day even warmer.

Or maybe it was her strained nerves that were overheating.

Up until now, self-preservation had deemed it necessary she ignore Memphis James's return to town. But today's tabloid article about Dalton and his fiancée had garnered Kate no less than eight sympathetic glances, three well-intentioned condolence hugs and one unsolicited pep talk from a bitter divorceé—all while simply waiting in line at the local café. As the recent ex-wife of Miami's favorite homegrown politician, fading into the background was impossible for Kate, especially with a heavy social schedule looming ahead. And for the first time since she'd started dating Dalton at sixteen, she was faced with the prospect of attending an event by herself.

The pitying looks she'd received from complete strangers were bad enough, but the public scrutiny was bound to get worse. Imagine how awful the tabloid headlines would be if she showed up at her high-school reunion alone?

Former Prom Queen Jilted by Her One-time King
Spurned Kate Anderson Attends Reunion Solo

Inhaling a calming breath, she forced her muscles to relax and renewed her resolve to ask Memphis for help, even if he was her childhood nemesis turned hot-shot stuntman...and a living reminder of the biggest mistake of her life. Apprehension threatened to crack her composure, and she stared up at the window far above the ground.

Where was the condolence hug when you *really* needed one?

There was a crackle of walkie-talkies from the crew on the street, and Kate caught her breath. One second later the window exploded, glass fragments spraying outward and fanning around the stuntman's form, Memphis following a graceful descending arc before plummeting toward the bone-breakingly hard, air-bag-less pavement below.

Kate's mouth turned to dust, her heart turned to stone and her every cell froze as, for several terrifying seconds, Memphis free-fell past twenty-one rows of windows. At the last possible moment the cable slowed his fall until he came to a jerky stop, just inches from the camera trained up at him from the ground.

Applause broke out around her. Dizzy, Kate sucked in a fortifying breath while her heart pulsed back to life, pounding with the aftereffects of an adrenaline surge so strong it had surely melted her nervous system. Kate released the barricade, her palms slick, and tried to brush off the grains of sand that had embedded into her skin during her tight grip. And she watched in shocked annoyance as Memphis calmly and coolly disconnected his harness as the crowd continued their cheering.

He had plunged to the ground at high rates of speed while *she* had aged five years in the process.

Since the day her twin brother had befriended the then thirteen-year-old hellraiser, Memphis had elicited so many heart-pounding reactions in her body that if her nervous system ever burned out completely, ninety-nine percent of the blame belonged to Memphis.

When Kate spied him heading off she abruptly brought her doubts up short. Without a second thought, she rounded the barricade and strode toward his retreating, blue-jean-encased figure. His well-formed backside and powerful legs brought back memories she'd done her best to forget.

A shout of displeasure came from the security guard to her left, but she ignored it and called out, "Memphis!"

Either Memphis hadn't heard or chose to ignore her call, but more warning voices came as the crew and security began to target her more aggressively. Sensing time was running out, Kate broke into a brisk walk that bordered on a jog, her casual sundress flapping around her legs and her high-heeled sandals pinching her feet, as if to remind her they weren't intended for giving chase.

"Memphis, wait!" she called again.

This time Memphis came to a stop and turned

on his heel, and she knew the second he recognized her. For a brief moment, his expression froze. The reaction stopped Kate in her tracks, a mere ten feet from the man who was looking at her with those mesmerizing caramel-colored eyes...

Like a movie special effect, immediately she was transported back five years to the last time they'd been together. She had just yelled at him to get out of her brother's hospital room. A yell fueled by fear for Brian, fury at Memphis and confusion at the memory of him making love to her in a fit of passion that had stripped her of the ability to function. Too bad the feel-good heights had been followed by the inevitable crash.

Dizzying emotional highs and death-defying lows.

Ecstasy and disaster.

Memphis never brought about humdrum emotions, and she needed to remember that truth. But her body was too busy appreciating the light brown, casually cut hair that blatantly defied refined society, the melt-in-your-mouth, thickly fringed eyes and the hard, masculine jaw that was sexily covered in half a day's growth. His walking, talking, sex-on-two-legs attitude had intimidated her as a teen and aroused her as a young adult.

For a moment she questioned the sanity of her plan. Maybe attending the social events alone and exposing herself to more public ridicule was the better option.

A security guard grabbed her arm, his gruff voice unhappy as he said, "You can't be back here, miss."

But Kate dug in her heels and didn't budge, her gaze locked on Memphis.

Memphis raised a hand. "Let her go, Hal," he said, his gaze targeting hers as he walked closer, her heart pumping harder with his every step.

"You know her?" the security guard said.

A half smile curled the corner of Memphis's lips with a familiar teasing humor, his sheer sex appeal cutting all the way to Kate's heart. "Yeah," Memphis said, coming to a stop four feet away. "I know her very well."

It was the slight emphasis on the word *very* that infused Kate with warmth, and her palms—already damp from the hair-raising fall and the hell-raising man before her—grew even more damp, remembering the passion. The *pleasure*...

Quietly inhaling another calming breath, Kate pulled a hand wipe infused with organic lavender from the travel container she kept in her purse. Shake enough hands during a campaign and later as a representative's wife and you learn to carry the necessary accoutrements. The ritual was soothing. Calming. And a vast improvement over the lingering grit on her palms left from the barricade. With the heated way Memphis was looking at her, a cold hosing-off was in order, but cooling her hands was the best she could do.

For a brief moment the apprehension returned, and she fought back the certainty that he'd never agree to her plan. She knew from personal experience that Memphis James did what Memphis James wanted. He always had and always would. Getting him to cooperate was going to require every ounce of the diplomatic skills she'd honed through the years.

As the daughter and granddaughter of two political giants, and a political ex-wife, God knows she'd had plenty of practice engaging in small talk. And given her history with the man in front of her, keeping the conversation superficial seemed wise.

She glanced up at the high-rise. "I see your death wish is still intact," she said lightly.

He sounded amused. "If I had a death wish I would have jumped without the cable."

"I heard you did while making the movie *The Indestructibles*."

"That was a special circumstance," he said.

"Special as in 'crazier than usual'?"

He lifted a shoulder nonchalantly. "All in a day's work."

"Jumping off tall buildings? Leaping out of helicopters?" She lifted a brow. "Driving cars off *cliffs?*"

Good God, when Kate had finally watched that much-anticipated stunt on the big screen, her heart had stopped during the slow-motion scene.

Memphis's brow bunched in amusement, and his voice held more than its fair share of suggestion. "You following my career, Angel Face?"

The nickname struck her hard, and emotion

punted the protest from her lips. "Please," she said, the light tone now a struggle to maintain. "Don't call me that." She'd hated his name for her as a teen, and had even more reason to despise the label today.

"Well," he said, an amused sparkle in those sinful eyes. "Angel Face fitted the placid, rule-obsessed girl you used to be." And then his gaze flared with a fire that sparked through the air and lit an unwelcome blaze in her, too. He stepped closer, looking down at her with the knowledge of a man who knew all her secrets, his rumbling voice loaded with memory. "But I guess we both know at least one incident where the nickname doesn't fit."

Fighting for calm, she sent him what she hoped was her legendary campaign-cool smile. "Angel Face didn't suit me nearly as much as Devil did you." It was time to set the ground rules of their new relationship. They were both adults, certainly they could move beyond the past to a more...sedate friendship.

One could only hope.

"So forget about coming on to me, Memphis," she went on firmly, ignoring the disturbing sensation his proximity created. "I'm not that easily intimidated teen anymore. The years have taught me how to maintain a certain amount of grace and dignity, no matter the adversity." A humiliating tabloid-dissected divorce had helped, as well.

"Are you referring to me?" he said.

"Yes," she said. "You take pride in being as adverse as possible."

"A guy has to be known for something," he said easily. "Is that why you're here, to put your new skills to the test?"

"It's an unfortunate perk," she said. "I'm here because I need your help."

The surprised scoff was sharp. "My help?" He stared at her for a moment, and then the hint of a teasing grin reappeared. "The circumstances must be dire for the mighty Kate Anderson to request assistance from little ol' me."

The soft Southern twang he reverted to when irritated, or aroused, only made his already rough voice sexier. The small knot of anxiety in Kate's stomach bloomed bigger, and she licked her lips. It was a risk pinning her hopes on the wildly unpredictable Memphis.

But which was worse? Suffering through more of the humiliating public sympathy that, deep down, she knew she mostly didn't deserve? Or enduring the taunting tone of the only man outside her marriage who knew why?

"Why are you coming to me for a favor?" Memphis crossed his arms across a well-cut chest, and his biceps bulged beneath his T-shirt, momentarily throwing Kate's concentration. "Is Armageddon upon us?" he said wryly. "Is the end of civilization at hand?"

"It is according to the man holding the sign on the corner of Fifth and Main," she said, striving for a nonchalant tone. "But on the off chance that doesn't pan out, my ten-year high-school reunion is a month away. And there are several pre-reunion functions that I don't want to attend alone."

Memphis tipped back his head and let out a genuine laugh. Yes, compared to the end of days her predicament did seem rather trite. But right now the doomsday feeling was real.

"The solution seems simple to me," he said. "Just don't go."

"I have to attend," she said. "I'm in charge. I've been working on this reunion for the past year." As chairwoman of the event she'd spent months coping with her isolation and loneliness by stressing over every detail. She had no choice. "Skipping out isn't an option."

"I guess it never occurred to you to go alone," he said, and his voice lowered a notch. "Or is Kate Anderson still unable to show her face in public without an adoring sap on her arm?"

The critique stung. "I don't need adoration."

"You certainly were on the receiving end of plenty in high school."

"I just want company." She inhaled a breath, struggling for calm. "Who I go with doesn't matter."

"Just a hint, Angel Face." Amused, he tipped his head, as if sharing a secret. "That's no way to make a guy feel special."

"You aren't special," she said lightly. "You're trouble."

His brow bunched together with exaggerated

concern. "Clearly you need to work on your dating techniques," he said. "I prefer to be wooed."

"Wooed?" she said, struggling to maintain her composure. "This won't be a date. You'd simply be attending as my friend."

His eyebrow climbed meaningfully. "Except, I'm not your friend."

"You are my *brother's* friend and I'm asking for a favor."

Two heartbeats passed before he said, "I guarantee you, Kate." His eyes grew dark with an emotion that left her spinning. "You don't want my help."

She steeled herself against his sensually teasing tone. By the look on his face it was clear he showed no signs of relenting, and her anxiety edged higher. With Memphis accompanying her, no one would dare lecture her about moving on from being the discarded wife. "I'm asking nicely, Memphis." She tried not to sound as desperate as she felt, digging deep for the Anderson smile that she'd perfected from an early age. "I just need a little of your time," she said, laying a hand on his arm.

The muscles beneath her fingers bunched, and the last trace of teasing amusement in his eyes died. A myriad of expressions flitted across his face, none of them obvious. But when he spoke, his voice was resigned.

"Sorry. You'll have to find another guy to parade around town," he said, and then he turned and headed for the crew gathered around a monitor, watching a replay of his spectacular fall.

Kate followed him. "There isn't anyone else."

He kept his eyes forward. "Where are all your groupies from that expensive private high school you attended?"

"I didn't have groupies."

"Okay, I stand corrected," he said, and then he glanced down at Kate. Unfortunately those long legs of his kept right on going, forcing her high-heeled sandals to double as track shoes. "Perhaps *flock of admirers* is a better phrase?" he went on.

"I didn't have those, either."

He let out an amused laugh. "That's not how I remember it. What I remember is a straitlaced, popular princess who attended the high school with the highest per-capita-income area code in the state, Biscayne Bay Preparatory Academy." He stopped and stepped close, and Kate's discomfort stepped up a notch, too. "A girl who was too good to give the time of day to a kid from lowly County High on the seedier side of town."

Heat crept up Kate's face. As a teen, there had been a whole host of reasons why Kate had treated her brother's best friend with a nonchalant reserve. Money had never entered her extensive list. "Your memory is jaded, Memphis."

He cocked his head, staring down at her with the look of a man who wasn't going to play along. "My memory is fine. It's your perception that's off." His eyes lingered on her face, and a combination of desire and dread tap-danced across her chest. "Then again," he went on softly, "burying your head in the sand was always your specialty."

By God, her marriage had proved that right.

But if she stopped to list all her mistakes she'd never get anything done. "I didn't come to discuss the past, Memphis."

He took a stray lock of her hair between his fingers, absently rubbing the strands, the back of his beautifully muscled forearm millimeters from her breast. "It doesn't work that way, Angel Face," he murmured. Her body throbbing, she blinked back the disturbing emotions, careful to keep her face blank. His all-seeing eyes held hers as he went on, his voice reflective. "Yesterday is inextricably linked to tomorrow via that inconvenient concept we call today."

He toyed with her hair a moment longer before dropping his hand.

She hated sounding desperate, but her tone came close to crossing that line. "I need your help, Memphis." She paused before going on. "Please."

For a fraction of a second he looked as if he cared that she was almost begging him. A muscle in his jaw ticked. "Why?"

How to explain to a man who could never relate? "Today I was forced to listen to a divorceé give a detailed description of how her sex life improved after her lousy husband dumped her, and then she proceeded to inform me to get back on the horse before it was too late."

His eyes crinkled in humor. "Sound advice."

A skeptical scoff escaped her lips. "I'm growing weary of all the advice."

"She was just offering you her sympathy."

"I don't need sympathy."

"Yeah. And I'm not sure you deserve it, either," he said thoughtfully, and a surge of guilt threatened to swamp her. But she pretended not to know what he was talking about when he went on. "Don't you have any friends you could ask?"

"No one who is available."

"Everything is for sale in this day and age," he said easily. "How about an escort service?"

She forced a patient look on her face. "I'm not hiring an escort."

His eyes crinkled in amusement. "It would come with some pretty powerful perks."

Kate pressed her lips together and counted to five, reminding herself that Memphis did whatever Memphis wanted. And right now it was clear he was intent on making her pay for the past.

Kate briefly closed her eyes, inhaling deeply and seeking a peaceful calm, not the turbulent chaos that he specialized in eliciting. "I'm not looking for perks."

Several seconds passed before he said, "Sorry, Kate." He almost sounded as though he meant it. "I am not going to be your go-to patsy." A hard glint flickered through his eyes. "I fell for your damsel-in-distress routine before, and I'm not doing it again."

She ignored the old shame and concentrated on today's humiliation instead. She had one trick left to get Memphis to agree. Her name was firmly attached to this reunion and, if nothing else, she would make sure it went off successfully.

"Brian told me you'd refuse," Kate said. At the mention of her brother, Memphis froze, his face devoid of emotion. The pause was the most awkward to date which, given their history, was saying something. "He asked me to tell you to consider saying yes as a favor to him."

Memory torqued his every muscle, and Memphis's body tensed as he remembered the last time he'd seen Kate, right outside Brian's hospital room. It was the only time in their history he'd seen her so tenaciously outspoken, not to mention *livid,* fighting for what she wanted. The feisty female he'd sensed all along but had rarely seen.

Until today.

Apparently the change was now permanent, and Memphis wondered how much their history together had contributed.

For the first time since she'd chased him down Memphis allowed himself a moment to take in every detail. The sleek blond hair was arranged in a loop at the back of her neck, a style that was casual yet elegant. A few loose tendrils framed her face. The blue eyes were clear and cool—and used to flip-flop between an infuriatingly eager-to-please manner toward her family and the frustrating ice-princess look of disapproval she'd saved for Memphis. Especially while lecturing him after every stunt he and her brother pulled as teenagers. And then there was the slim figure in a classy sundress that covered her gentle curves, a sight that could tempt a man into doing things he knew wouldn't turn out well for him. A body that in one memorable night had ferried Memphis straight to heaven right before it had condemned him to hell.

Memphis cleared his throat, sorry all the memories weren't as easy to banish. "How is Brian?"

"He's getting around better now," Kate said, the words expanding the uneasiness in his gut. For a moment her expression softened. "You should give him a call."

Regret made his voice gruffer than he'd planned. "Eventually."

There was an awkward pause before she went on. "Well," Kate said. "Will you help me?"

He'd rather face the harrowing drop he'd done off the rim of the Grand Canyon last year, the one that had come close to getting him killed. All for an action film remembered only for its death-defying stunts by Memphis James and its lethal lack of a decent script.

Memphis ruffled an impatient hand through his hair, studying Kate. His teasing, provoking behavior in the past had all been in response to a teenage obsession that had frustrated the heck out of him. Fortunately, hellaciously sharp chemistry aside, experience had made him immune to her now. But Kate had definitely changed, correctly surmising the one weakness he had left and using it against him—which meant he was caught between the woman he'd sworn off long ago and the friend to whom he owed a debt that could never be repaid.

Helping Brian's sister was the least he could do.

"Okay," he said, letting out his breath and giving one last swipe through his hair. "I'll do it." He dropped his hand to his side. "Exactly what does this favor entail?"

"In celebration of completing our task, the reunion committee has voted to combine business with pleasure," she said. "There are several meetings that have been turned into social functions."

"Sounds like the kind of pompous crap your private-school classmates would pull," he muttered.

"I want you to go with me," she said.

He narrowed his eyes at her, growing wary. "How many events?"

Dropping her gaze to his shoulder, she fingered the belt of her dress, and her uneasy fidgeting didn't bode well for Memphis. "A dinner party, three cocktail parties..." Kate met his gaze again. "And then there are the two events on the reunion weekend itself."

Memphis's mind balked at the thought. "No wonder you can't find anyone to help you. I'll agree to the dinner party and one cocktail party." He shot her a you're-crazy look. "But I didn't attend Biscayne Bay Preparatory Academy. No way am I going to your reunion."

"But that's the main event I don't want to attend alone."

Memphis enunciated each word succinctly. "I am not going to your reunion." Brian's old classmates would take one look at Memphis and remember his highly publicized mistake. The one that had almost killed his friend... "That's beyond the kind of torture I can take. You'll have to find someone else for that phase of your plan."

Kate blew out a breath and eyed him steadily. "One dinner party, *two* cocktail parties, and the reunion weekend," she said, going on smoothly. "Brian will be there, and he's looking forward to seeing you."

Damn, another low blow. "One reunion event," he said, hating that he'd caved in the face of her less-than-subtle pressure. "Either Friday or Saturday. Your choice."

"Deal," she said, and then her eyes swept down his well-worn jeans. "And I get to select the clothes you wear."

The grin hit him hard, as did her sweeping gaze. "You got a problem with my wardrobe?"

She lifted a brow. "I remember what you wore after one of my misguided classmates invited you to our prom."

"Tiffany Bettingfield didn't mind my faded kakis and athletic shoes. Because after I watched you get crowned Prom Queen alongside your golden-boy Prom King—" his smile crept higher "—Tiffany suggested we head to my car. I was happy to show her that there are more important things about a man than his clothes."

"Hopefully she's recovered from her lapse in judgment by now," she said with a sarcasm that was so smooth he almost missed the tone. "Do we have a deal?"

Despite everything, Memphis was delighted with Kate Anderson's new spunk wrapped in her usual class. "Deal," he confirmed. "But just to be clear, I'm doing this for Brian, not you."

Her lips twisted. "Don't worry, Memphis. I'm under no illusions you would ever do a favor for me."

A sliver of anger shot through him, momentarily dimming his good humor. There was a time in his teens when he'd have done anything for Kate, if she'd only hinted that she cared. But those days were long gone, killed in a fateful night that had had far-reaching consequences that neither of them could have predicted.

Her ice-princess behavior and hands-off attitude used to frustrate the hell out of him, but these days things were different. He was certainly done touching Kate, but now he was impressed and intrigued by her cool demeanor and polite facade, especially in the face of their tumultuous past.

Yet a small part of him longed to see her emotional cool crack, just for a moment. And, after their teen years, provoking her was as ingrained as breathing.

"I did you a favor once." He deliberately turned his voice husky. "Do you remember?"

He took comfort in the slight catch of her breath, a small smile forming on his lips as Kate clearly struggled to remain composed.

"Memphis," she finally said, recovering her cool and holding his gaze. "That was a long time ago. And even *you* can't be so conceited as to think of sex as a favor."

He studied her for a moment and then he leaned close, inhaling the haunting scent of lavender he'd come to equate with Kate. "Well, it ranked right up there as one of the best nights of my life," he murmured, and the bitter truth in his teasing words made his smile grow tight. "Right up until I found out you and Dalton were still married."

CHAPTER TWO

GUILT.

Kate closed her eyes as her heart strained to keep from crumpling under the weight of the emotion. She'd let the feeling drive her back to a marriage that had begun to die long before the night she'd spent in Memphis's arms. And then she'd let the emotion keep her stuck in her vow of forever well beyond the point where all hope for a happy-from-here-on-out was gone.

But there was only so much guilt a girl could take before she eventually was either permanently crippled by it or finally declared she was moving on. And the time for that was now, if for no other reason than to save her sanity.

She lifted her lids and said the words that were five years overdue. "I'm sorry."

Too bad the apology didn't make her feel any better.

"Sorry?" He tipped his head skeptically, as if vaguely amused by her pitiful words. "For which part? For leaving without saying goodbye? Or for me learning the truth from your brother?"

Her heart stopped. "You called Brian?"

"The very next day," he said. "And in an attempt to figure out what the hell had just happened, I casually asked him how you were doing." He lifted an eyebrow. "Imagine my surprise when he said you were having marital problems."

Heart now doing double time, Kate pressed her lips together and blindly turned to look at the dwindling crowd, but she was determined to keep moving forward. Growing up in the spotlight—with every family problem scrutinized by the public in excruciating detail—had taught her to persevere. Pretending everything was okay wasn't always the best choice, but sometimes it was the only one you had.

"The first function is this weekend." She faced Memphis again. "We need to make plans."

He shot her an incredulous look.

"Part of the deal was I'd help you pick out something suitable to wear," she went on.

After a brief hesitation, his lips twitched. "I'm sure I can find something appropriate in my closet," he said, the look in his eyes one of pure entertainment.

At her expense, of course.

Clearly her soundness of mind was taking a brief holiday. After all, she'd convinced Memphis to spend the next month helping her. She was going to need a straitjacket before this was over, mostly to keep from pulling her hair out in frustration.

"You forget," she said, feigning patience. "I've seen your idea of appropriate."

"Fine," he said, startling her with his easy agreement. Grateful he'd given in so easily, she let her tensed muscles relax, until he jerked his head in the direction of the street. "Let's go," he said.

"Where?"

"To check out my wardrobe."

"Now?" Her heart sank and the tension returned. She hadn't even *begun* to recover from seeing him again.

"No time like the present." He sent her a tiny smile that left her hugely nervous. "You can follow me home and check out the contents of my closet."

Still questioning her good sense, Kate followed Memphis into the upmarket apartment in an exclusive neighborhood, noting that he was all but ignoring her as she trailed behind him into the kitchen. The lack of attention was a welcome change. He tossed his keys on the kitchen table and turned to lean a hip against the counter, watching her as she assessed what was clearly meant to be temporary living quarters.

In one slow pivot she took in the kitchen and the spartanly furnished living area. A flat-screen TV, a single leather recliner and a side table were the extent of the furniture. No couch. No bookshelves. The walls were painted white, and there were no pictures or mementos to break up the bland color theme. The apartment was a blank slate waiting for the occupant to fill it with his belongings, bringing a personal touch.

Memphis hadn't bothered.

"It could do with a little sprucing up," she said. It was then she noticed several framed photographs on the floor, propped against the wall as if it was too much trouble to hang them in place.

For a moment he looked as if he regretted letting her come to check out his wardrobe. "My needs are simple," he said.

"I can see you have a love of basic white," she said dryly.

"Even if I was into interior decorating, which I'm not, I'm not in town long enough to bother," he said. "It has everything I need: a great location, a refrigerator…" The only movement was a slight tip of the head. "And a bed."

The silence that followed filled the room, his expression remarkably placid, no overt twinkle in his gaze necessary. The thick, dark eyelashes gave him a sinfully sated look, framing caramel-colored eyes that oozed sex, whether intentional or not.

She knew he'd brought her here to make her uncomfortable, and the sooner she got this over with the sooner she'd get out of his apartment. Her heart was pounding embarrassingly fast, and no matter how many lectures she'd given herself as she'd followed him here, it was hard not to remember the last time they'd been alone together in an apartment. Completing her task and getting out of his home suddenly became a top priority.

But clothes meant closets, and closets meant bedrooms, and suddenly her heart stopped and she couldn't breathe.

Stalling for time to recuperate from his effect on her, she crossed to the living room and picked up one of the pictures. It was of a red convertible Porsche, top back as it sailed off the end of a towering cliff. Like a surfer, Memphis was crouched on the driver seat, his hand on the top of the windshield, body poised to push off.

She wasn't a fan of action movies, but when the film had been released Kate had gone to see it in the theatre. Alone in the dark, with only her popcorn for company, she'd watched the hero— who, in actuality, had been Memphis—push off from the free-falling car and do a back flip in the air before unfolding into position. Arms pressed to his side, body arrow-straight to decrease wind resistance, he'd aimed for the flatbed truck far, far below. At the last possible second he'd pulled the cord to the chute on his back and targeted the moving semi, landing gracefully on the trailer.

The stunt had brought back all the turbulent emotions Memphis had elicited as a teen, the larger-than-life adolescent constantly goading her into feelings that were too messy to handle. Exasperation. Danger. And a whole lot of electric chemistry that had short-circuited her ability to function when he was near. Back then, Dalton had made her feel safe.

But the only reason she'd been watching Memphis's stunt on screen was because her husband had backed out on his date night with her. Just another one of many nights she'd spent by herself, achingly lonely because Dalton had been buried in his studies at law school. Not the happy marriage she'd envisioned when he'd proposed. But how could she fault him for fulfilling the dreams she had staunchly supported from the beginning? So she'd headed to the theatre alone. At the last second, she chose Memphis's latest movie instead of the indie film she'd planned.

And she'd spent the rest of the night with vivid dreams, relieving the adolescent angst and the clashing attraction she'd worked so hard to keep under wraps.

Memphis's voice came from behind. "That was my first big film."

Disturbed by his nearness, she gripped the picture frame. "How did you get your start?"

"BASE jumping."

Ignoring the heat from his body, she kept her gaze on the photo. "I never understood the appeal the sport held for you and Brian. Is skydiving from an airplane too tame?"

"A bit too regimented for my taste. Where's the illicit fun in that?"

"Illegal or not, I'm not sure there is any fun to be had while free-falling toward earth," she said, and finally turned her face to brave a look at him. "But I don't understand how BASE jumping led to your career."

"The second unit director of my first paid stunt, a low-budget film, just happened to be wandering by when I jumped from an antennae tower in Hollywood. A friend had to give him my name because, when I landed, I was too busy running from the security guard."

She lifted a brow. "The authorities don't look too kindly on people trespassing."

"Like I said, it's no fun unless there is an element of danger."

"Yes," she said with barely restrained sarcasm. "Because plummeting toward earth at high rates of speed isn't dangerous enough."

He stepped around her, leaning his back against the wall, the indolent pose made all the more sensual by the lean muscle in his arms and in the thighs beneath his jeans. "There is a crazy system in the stunt business. You have to be ballsy, but not *too* ballsy. Four out of five and you're crazy enough to do anything required to get the job done. When you hit five…" He lifted a shoulder and stared at her with a trace of amusement. "When you get to five you're just too crazy to deal with on the set."

Crazy sounded right.

Kate tipped her head. "Which one are you?"

His trace of a grin grew bigger. "Depends on who you ask."

Chaos. Disarray. Memphis's life had always been notably fraught with disorder, not to mention danger. It was just one of many reasons why Kate's parents had forbidden her brother from being his friend. Not that Brian had ever followed the rules, either.

Avoiding his gaze, she ran a hand along the smooth edge of the picture frame, fighting back the memories of a passion the likes of which she had never known before nor experienced since. The messy, chaotically electric feelings overwhelmed her in every sense of the word. Their exhilarating night had marked the midway point in her bleak, eight-year marriage, leaving Kate more alive in that moment than in the four years preceding or the four years after.

"How long will you be around?" she said. She hoped the question came out as simple civil conversation instead of real curiosity.

"As short a time as humanly possible."

For some reason, his response bothered her, and she lifted her gaze to meet his. "Are you in that much of a hurry to leave?"

Memphis let out a sharp bark of a humorless laugh. "As far as I'm concerned, there aren't enough stunts like the one I did today. I took the job despite the fact it meant returning to Miami."

"I heard your parents moved."

"I bought them a place in California several years ago, so there's nothing left for me here."

She ignored the obvious fact that Brian lived here. That Kate Anderson didn't factor into his equation was no surprise.

"Where is home now?" she said.

"Wherever my next big gag is scheduled to take place."

"Gag?" she asked, confused by the unfamiliar term.

"Stunt," he clarified.

"Do you plan to keep up this nomadic existence forever?" She narrowed her eyes doubtfully. "And just what is your long-term career goal, outside of being labeled the man who never says no to leaping off tall buildings?"

"To be the best damn high-fall stuntman in Hollywood."

She studied him for a moment. "And when does that happen?"

He stared at her, and, although his posture was relaxed, uncaring, the intensity in his eyes gave him away. "When everyone knows my name," he said, as if the simple statement justified his insane job.

Before she could ask any more questions, he nodded in the direction of the hallway. "If you want to check out my clothes you'll have to go to my closet," he said, sending her belly BASE jumping for her toes, those sinfully sexy eyes far too steady on hers. "My bedroom is at the end of the hallway."

The mood grew strained as Memphis followed Kate down the corridor. His chest grew tight, a potent mix of desire, tension and a touch of self-directed frustration snaking around his rib cage. His bedroom was just as barren as the living area, except for the king-size bed that was currently commanding center stage like a mocking reminder of their past.

He'd sworn off touching Kate again, but right now her delicate scent was filling every corner of the room where he slept. And suddenly, her presence in his personal space made him uncomfortably aware his vow of keeping his hands to himself might be harder to pull off than he'd thought.

"Everything is in the closet," he said.

Kate looked around the almost empty room. "You don't have a dresser?"

"The rental apartment didn't come with one."

She shot him a look. "And you couldn't be bothered with buying a few pieces of furniture?"

"What would be the point? I arranged only for what I absolutely needed because I'm not going to be around long enough for it to matter."

He had no intention of discussing just how hard he'd grappled with the decision to return to his hometown. It was the only place his reputation as a high-fall stuntman was ever called into question. Granted, his mistake had been five years ago, and had taken place during a prank. But still...

The five-year-old ache of regret resurfaced and he pushed it aside, refusing to dwell on the role this woman had played in that moment, as well.

And if he had to spend the next month attending one pretentious social function after another, he might as well indulge in his favorite pastime from his teens: provoking Kate, if for no other reason than to arouse some kind of emotion from her. And it had nothing to do with caring why she kept herself so carefully contained.

Not only was he done touching Kate, he was done wondering why she tried so hard to keep her emotions encased in ice.

She opened the doors to the walk-in closet, staring inside, and Memphis bit back the urge to smile as a look of dismay slowly spread across her face.

The jeans and shirts on the shelves were haphazardly arranged—okay, "hastily dumped" was probably a better description. And he had better clothes at home, but why cart them along for a month's worth of work?

Kate finally turned a doubtful face to Memphis.

He gave an easy shrug, amused by her expression. "I travel light."

Her lips quirked at the understatement. "There must be something usable in here."

"Nothing that will fit the Anderson norm, for sure," he said with a hint of humor, running his gaze down her form.

Although her sundress was simple and modest, nothing come-hither about it, the dress also reeked of wealth and privilege. As always, she was meticulously put together. And the exposed creamy skin of her shoulders was tempting him to take a taste.

"If by 'Anderson norm' you mean an occasional article outside of denim," she said with an overly patient look, turning her attention back to the shelves. "You'd be right."

"Nothing wrong with denim."

"There is when it's all you have."

"For a former representative's wife, I suppose you're right." He shot her a skeptical look. "But I don't give a damn about standards."

"That's not true." She pulled out a pair of jeans and shook them out, staring at the holes in the knees. "What I remember is a boy who went out of his way to defy every standard society threw in his direction." And the look she sent him challenged him to disagree.

Humor tugged at the corner of his lips. "I think you mistake me for someone who cared."

His family might have been poor, but he was comfortable with his simple beginnings. Proud of where he'd come from and what he'd made of himself. He didn't give a damn about people's perception of him now, and he'd been even less concerned way back when. As a teen, the only exception to that rule had been the disapproving looks on Kate's face.

Those had irked the hell out of him.

"I think you cared very much about helping Brian annoy my parents," she said.

He fought back the surge of resentment. "Oh, come on, Kate. Face it," he said. "It wouldn't have mattered what I did. The ugly truth is your parents hated me. Still do, truth be told."

Jeans clutched in her fingers, she dropped her hands to her waist. "They didn't hate you," she said with an exaggerated show of patience, though there was a hint of a defensive tone. "They simply—" She paused, as if to find the right words, and refolded the pants into a neat little bundle, placing them back on the shelf. "They were worried about your influence on Brian."

The delicate phrasing brought a small scoff of irony. "They were more concerned about the neighborhood I lived in and the risk I'd contaminate their only son."

When she turned with protest in her eyes, he shot her a half grin and crossed the room to lean against the doorjamb. Near enough to smell her scent, to touch her skin. And there was a lot of skin exposed in that pretty little slip of a sundress, demure or not.

If he couldn't get her aroused, he'd have to get her annoyed. He supposed the partial grin on his face might have been a touch predatory. "Though they should have been worrying I'd contaminate their perfect darling of a teenage daughter."

Hesitation rolled off her like sweat from a newbie poised to leap from a skyscraper, until she straightened those tempting shoulders, her blue eyes recovering their cool. "There was never any risk of that."

Another amused scoff burst from his mouth. "I remember the heat that sizzled between us every time you showed up to coolly give me a piece of your mind."

"That was anger."

"That was lust."

Her brow crinkled with disagreement. "I was just a kid."

"You were a half-grown woman." The words came out throatier than he would have liked. He hooked his thumbs through his belt loops and leaned in closer, catching a whiff of her scent. "You were turned on by the guy your parents would've never let you date. The chemistry was impressive."

"It's your *ego* that was impressive."

"With good reason."

"Always the hero in your own script," she drawled lightly.

Despite her light tone, her blue eyes bubbled with barely restrained emotions, yet he couldn't identify the first one. Memphis couldn't tell if she was disturbed by his nearness or irritated by his refusal to go along with her interpretation of the past. Time stretched until it grew uncomfortable, their history pulsing between them. In a space of a full ten seconds filled with desire, heat and intense pleasure, Memphis relived just how right this woman had felt in his arms. Although their moment hadn't come until long after their teens, he didn't trust the feeling, sure it was a figment of his lust-induced mind. His adolescent fantasy come to life.

How could she have felt anything but right when he'd spent years imagining how she would taste? And when she'd finally released all that careful restraint, it had been a life-changing experience that had caused him to doubt his instincts. Because in that moment it had felt as if she belonged to him....

He jerked his thoughts to a halt. Just who the hell was the real Kate?

She held his gaze, and he wondered if her cheeks were flushed from anger or desire. There was no answer. And when she turned back to straightening out the contents of his closet, Memphis watched in amazement as she reached for the next pair of holey jeans and refolded them, as well.

He studied her profile, her movements graceful and dignified even while performing a mundane task. "When you're done in here you can rearrange the dirty clothes in my hamper if you like," he said with a wry twist of his lips.

"No, thank you," she said smoothly as she continued with her self-appointed duties.

"And I have dirty dishes in the dishwasher that could use restacking according to size."

"I'm sure you're capable of handling that yourself."

"My underwear could use a good ironing, as well," he said.

Kate sent him a sharp look from the corner of her eye, but continued to fold his last pair of jeans, placing it in a neat line with the others.

"Angel Face, I hate to be the one to break the bad news," he said softly, but with no shortage of sarcasm. "But rearranging my clothes isn't going to change them into designer brands."

She picked up a T-shirt and began to fold it.

"I realize that," she said as, midtask, she faced him, her clear skin and high cheekbones capturing his gaze.

The regal set to her chin begged to be challenged with a kiss. And if he concentrated real hard, he'd remember that wasn't the job he'd signed on for.

Instead, he said, "I've always wanted to ask, is the politically correct Kate a fixed product of her family genes or just a result of her upbringing?"

"Neither." Her tone was cuttingly cool as she continued rearranging his T-shirts. "What you call political correctness the rest of the world calls being civil."

A laugh burst from his throat, and he swept a stray lock of wheat-colored hair from her bare shoulder, hoping for a reaction. Or at least to get her to stop organizing the contents of his closet.

"I can handle polite as long as it's some semblance of the truth." Frustration shifted his voice an octave lower. "But what I can't stand is when you bury your head in the sand and try to rewrite the truth."

She straightened the last T-shirt, the closet now tidy, and turned to face him, crossing her arms. But he wasn't sure if the posture was out of defiance or to shield herself from his proximity. "What truth am I trying to rewrite?"

"Your family." His gaze held hers. "The past." He paused and leaned in close, enjoying the look of discomfort on her face, even as his chest twisted at the haunting sight of her luscious lips. His voice came out low. "You and me."

She hesitated, blinked once, and then hiked a delicate brow. "I'm doing nothing of the sort."

Disappointed he hadn't gotten the slightest rise from her, he said, "Then what are you doing?"

"Concluding that you have nothing appropriate to wear."

He raised an eyebrow. "Am I supposed to care about that, too?"

"Not at all." The smooth smile on her face should have been a warning, and he barely withheld the groan when she shared her plan. "Because tomorrow we're going shopping."

CHAPTER THREE

"WELCOME, Mr. James." The redheaded clerk greeted him as if they were old friends, and Memphis's lips twitched at the irony. The saleslady then aimed her plastic smile at Kate. "It's lovely to see you again, Mrs. Worthington—"

"Anderson," Kate said smoothly. "It's Anderson now."

"Oh, yes. Of course." The hint of color on the clerk's face was the only sign of her blunder. "I forgot." The woman's eyes slid back to Memphis as she rounded the counter, clearly curious about their relationship but too well-trained to ask. "I'm pleased you scheduled time with us this afternoon," she said to Kate. "Why don't we discuss your wardrobe needs, and I'll see how I can help."

Help? Shopping wasn't on his list of enjoyable activities. But shopping with *two* women? Well...he didn't see how the experience could get much worse.

Except it did.

Since Memphis had first entered the designer-clothing store, approximately two seconds ago, he'd fought the urge to walk back out, leaving the endless stretch of gray marble, the high, wood-paneled ceiling and the subtle lighting. Years ago the clerk wouldn't have recognized his last name. So far Kate had gone by two, both of which commanded instant attention.

His lips twisted wryly. It had taken him thirty years to attain what she'd been granted simply by being born into one of Florida's most powerful political dynasties.

While the two women talked, Memphis glanced at the suits that lined the far wall and the tables and racks with shirts and pants on display. Each article of clothing was arranged with a total of lack of concern for efficient use of real estate, signifying just how high-end the South Beach, Miami, store was—and how much the clothes would cost. Nowadays Memphis could handle the expense with ease, but he still had a problem with the attitude.

The only reason the saleslady was being so solicitous was because of Kate's presence and his now mostly famous name.

"The VIP room is in the back." The clerk sent Memphis an assessing look, obviously liking what she saw, and his eyes crinkled in amusement. Okay, so maybe the woman appreciated more than his name. "You two can enjoy the refreshments in our fitting room while I do the selecting for you," the redhead finished.

"I think you and I should divide and conquer,"

Kate said to the clerk. "We have a lot of ground to cover."

Memphis winced and shifted on his feet, already impatient. "I'm perfectly capable of picking out my own clothes."

Capable, and a lot quicker than two choosy females.

"Remember our agreement?" Kate said, clearly biting back a smile. "I do the selecting."

Stifling the groan was difficult. "But I could have it done in five minutes."

"I booked the private fitting room for considerably longer," Kate said.

At her amused look, Memphis narrowed his eyes. Was trapping him in designer hell her way of paying him back for cornering her in the closet?

"And my time is a part of the service, Mr. James," the clerk said, interrupting his thoughts and turning her full-wattage smile on him. "I'll select a few suits appropriate for the formal event." After a lingering glance at Memphis, the clerk headed off.

"She looked eager to help," Kate murmured, clearly entertained as she watched the woman for a moment before turning to face Memphis.

His lips quirked. "*Eager* is a good description."

"I think she might even offer to undress you herself."

"Intriguing suggestion," he said dryly. "Though I doubt it would speed up this process."

"Obviously she's willing to go above and beyond the call of duty," she said, stepping closer to reach a rack of white dress shirts.

Which, unfortunately, brought her scent to his attention.

Last night his dreams of Kate had been the ultimate in erotic. It was easy to blame them on the lavender that lingered in the air in his home, or the memories of sparring with her in his closet, but Memphis knew better.

Though beyond tempting, it was best not to dwell on the dreams. He turned to eye the clothes on the rack beside them. "What is tomorrow night's dinner party for, anyway?"

"A pleasant way for the members of the reunion committee to celebrate while ironing out a few last-minute details," she said. Sliding the hangers on the rack of dress shirts, she studied each one critically in turn, taking a whole lot longer than he liked. "And discussing any updates that need to be made to our website," she said.

"You have a website?"

"Of course, it's the best way to find classmates and generate excitement about the event. Didn't you go to your ten-year reunion? It would have been, what...?" She paused, as if trying to remember, staring down at the shirt in her hand as if its selection was paramount to the future of the world. "Three years ago?"

"Two," he said. Growing impatient with her inspection of a simple shirt, he reached out and selected one from the rack. "I'm two years older than you and about a hundred years wiser."

Which seemed to sum up their relationship through the years.

She sent him an amused look, clearly disagreeing with his statement. "And how did you come to that conclusion?"

"Because no one in their right mind needs to sort through a rack of dress shirts where *every one* of them is white." He held up the one in his hand, his brow pinched with skepticism. "Outside of the correct size, what else is there to choose?"

She took the shirt from his clasp. "Cut. Style," she said patiently, but Memphis got the feeling it was a struggle for her. "The collar and the thread count, just to name a few." She lifted an eyebrow at him. "You want to be comfortable, don't you?"

"I won't be comfortable until these functions are behind me," he said with a small frown of frustration. "And who really cares what I'm wearing?"

"*You* should. As my companion, the press is likely to analyze and criticize your every move, including your choice of attire. Take it from someone who knows," she said. "You don't want to give them any ammunition beyond their own twisted imaginations."

She studied him for a moment before returning the shirt in her hand to the rack. And Memphis had the distinct impression he'd just taken a step backward in his mission to complete the afternoon of torture.

"Why did you put that one back?" he said with a groan.

"The fit will be wrong," she said. "You're in excellent shape, so you'll look best in a tailored style."

He picked up another shirt she'd rejected. "And what's wrong with this one?"

"The thread count. All other things being equal, the thread count is important in how it feels against your body." Obviously the skepticism rolled off him in discernible waves. She steadily held his gaze. "You don't believe me."

In answer, he simply hiked a brow.

She removed the two he'd selected from the rack and handed them back to him. "Okay," she said, holding up the ones she'd chosen. "Let's go take them all for a test drive." She bunched her brow in amusement and went on. "I bet you'll feel a difference."

"I bet you're wrong." He followed close behind as she headed for the private dressing room in back. "At least tell me you don't try to control the clothing of every guy you've dated since Dalton."

"I haven't been out on a date yet."

Stunned by the news, Memphis stopped short. Her ex was engaged, albeit at record speeds, but she hadn't even found the time to go out with another man. Kate must have sensed he was no longer following her, and she stopped and turned to face him.

He shouldn't be so curious. "Why not?"

"No time."

Memphis scanned her face, wondering what was stirring behind those blue eyes of hers, a disturbing thought working its way into his brain. "I hope that's not just an excuse because you're pining for your ex."

"Trust me, Memphis," she said, her lips twisting. "I'm not pining for a man."

Both relieved and disturbingly challenged by the news, Memphis leaned in close. "Not even for me?"

She blinked once as she met his eyes, the emotion unreadable. "Least of all you."

Although he'd started out teasing her, as Memphis stared at Kate's steady blue gaze, a small stab of resentment flared, and he struggled to tamp down the unwanted emotion in his chest. There was a time in his teens when he would have loved to have Kate pine for him, despite their age difference. And how could she throw herself so passionately into a night of making love with him only to go back and spend another four years with her husband? He sure as hell hadn't entered into the moment with forever in mind, but it still grated that she could nonchalantly walk away.

As if he were a dress shirt that wasn't suitable.

"Well," he said softly. "I know you like what I did to you." Her eyes widened a fraction, and he went on. "There's no denying that."

He enjoyed the way, these days, she held his gaze instead of visually scurrying for cover when confronted. But she didn't look quite as composed now, her breaths coming a little faster. Whether it was from attraction, nerves or irritation at his reminder of her less-than-noble moment, he wasn't sure.

"It was simply sex, Memphis," she said in a low voice.

"There was nothing simple about it."

She bit her lower lip. "That night had everything to do with my state of mind and nothing to do with you."

"It was *me* you wrapped your arms around while you cried."

"I'd had a huge fight with Dalton and left with the intention of never going back. I was looking for an escape from it all. I didn't expect to find you at my brother's apartment."

He paused, letting the memory wash over him. After years of being away from Miami, he'd been disappointed his friend was out of town, but crashing at Brian's place on his way through had only made sense. Until a sobbing Kate had let herself into her brother's apartment, so inconsolable she couldn't speak. Thrown by the sudden appearance of his old crush and disturbed by her profound sadness, he'd pulled her into his arms to console her. It was the first time he'd ever felt sorry for Kate Anderson.

And it would definitely be the last.

"I know you were upset, Angel Face." Although his voice was soft, he couldn't contain the edge to his tone. "But after twenty minutes of sobbing against my chest, when you'd finally recovered enough to speak, all you did was beg me to make love to you."

And in the span of a fleeting two seconds, he'd debated waiting until she was less emotional. A fleeting two seconds of brilliant insight that had been followed by hours of blissful—*pleasurable*—ignorance.

As the silence grew, tension infiltrated the air.

"Memphis..." Kate closed her eyes, and her voice grew wearily frustrated. "I made a mistake. All I can do is say I'm sorry. What else do you want from me?"

Edgy, feeling the sudden urge to leap off a tall building, he was beginning to realize he didn't know the answer to that question himself. He hated being considered a mistake. And what *did* he want? Another apology? A hundred of them? Or maybe a chance to prove she wasn't as delicious as he remembered...

He tamped down the thought. For now he'd settle for a little acknowledgment. Starting with the truth she dodged when convenient. All pretense and teasing gone, he said, "I want you to admit *out loud* that you wanted me that night as much as I wanted you."

She lifted her lids, the blue eyes troubled, but said nothing.

The need to hear the words grew more acute, and he shifted closer, determined to use any means necessary. "And when you spend the night with me again," he went on. "I'd prefer you didn't sneak away without saying goodbye."

Her mouth worked for a moment before she responded. "I won't sleep with you again."

Damn, he should be agreeing with her.

Why wasn't he agreeing with her?

Unfortunately, the only thing he wanted right now was to pull her into his arms and verify that she didn't taste as good as she did in his memories. Without pausing for a second thought, he reached for her, Kate's lids stretched wide in surprise—and they were interrupted by the red-headed sales lady.

"Here you two are." The clerk beamed at them as if she'd just bought the winning lottery ticket. "Follow me and I'll take you to the VIP room."

Still wobbly from the disturbing near-miss encounter, Kate gratefully sank into one of the copper-colored silk armchairs of the luxurious private fitting room as the salesclerk loaded the rack with their selections, along with her own. The large room came equipped with a well-stocked bar and an offering of gourmet cookies. The latter didn't interest Kate at all, but the former might come in handy before the afternoon was over.

The bumpy trip down memory lane had left her shaky. She'd spent the first two years of her marriage convincing herself time would make things better, and the second two years feeling neglected. Her fight that fateful night with Dalton had left her horribly confused and hopeless that things would ever improve. She'd needed to feel that she was important to him. He'd needed her to accept the life of sacrifice as a future politician's wife. Going to her parents afterward to confess her relationship was over had been a mistake, because they'd simply said that marriage was hard, Dalton was a good man and to go back to her husband. In that moment, she'd never felt more alone. Brian's company would have helped.

Memphis had been a dangerous substitute.

"I don't know why I'm going along with this," Memphis muttered as he stood in the center of the dressing room, as if unclear exactly why he was still here.

Kate pushed the memories aside and crossed her legs. "Just start with trying on a few shirts," she said. "It can't be near as bad as hitting an air bag from a hundred-foot drop—"

Memphis pulled his T-shirt over his head—cutting her sentence short—and tossed the garment aside. Kate was grateful she was already sitting. Now clad in nothing but jeans, Memphis's form elicited a full-scale assault on her senses. The vision of a lean, muscle-adorned chest brought back a slew of powerful memories....

Memphis, frowning as he finally relented to her pleas and claimed her mouth with his.

Her, beneath him, clinging to his hard torso as passion drove away the years of loneliness.

"Can I get you anything from the bar, Ms. Anderson?" the clerk said. Now that Memphis was shirtless, the woman's voice sounded strained.

Kate blinked, and the vision of a bare-chested Memphis returned. A drink? Absolutely. An alcoholic beverage was definitely in order.

Kate sent the saleslady a beyond-grateful smile. "What do you have?"

"Champagne." The redhead's gaze slid to Memphis, and she looked as if she needed a drink too. "We also carry a nice selection of wine and several imported beers."

"Wine," Kate said. "Red, please."

The saleslady complied, and as she poured the drink Memphis said, "She's a lightweight, so I wouldn't be too liberal with my portions."

Kate shot him a look. Memphis obviously felt no need to send the saleslady away, and the clerk was clearly loath to leave. Kate was simply glad the woman provided a buffer, so she accepted the glass with a smile. After a sip that curled low in her belly, she took another—all in the name of fortification, of course—and sent the saleslady a bigger smile.

"Have a seat and we can rate the selections," Kate said.

The clerk's return grin was brilliant as she complied. "If you insist."

Kate glanced at the masculine chest on display and restrained the sigh. "Might as well enjoy your job," she muttered.

"Some days are definitely better than others," the clerk murmured.

Memphis headed for the rack, the corded muscles and sinew in his back rippling as he shifted through the selections.

Eyes on the vast expanse of masculinity on display—and trying hard not to remember how long she'd gone without—Kate picked up the basket of cookies, offering the clerk one. "If you can't have wine, at least enjoy a baked good."

Kate turned and saw the clerk was just as pleased with the view.

"I probably should," the redhead said. "I think my blood sugar just dropped." Her smile was wan. "I'm feeling a little woozy."

As if oblivious, Memphis turned and lifted his arms over his head, spearing them into the sleeves of a dress shirt, the muscles in his chest shifting. Kate heard the clerk catch her breath at the beautiful display that highlighted his athleticism, his power and his dedication to his job by how meticulously he maintained his physical condition. And with the sexily rumpled style of his brown hair, Memphis always looked as if he'd just climbed out of bed after enjoying a satisfying night....

Kate briefly pressed her lids closed. Dear God, maybe that perception was more a reflection of her than him. She took another gulp of wine that her hit her empty stomach and burned, the warmth spreading lower.

Shirt now buttoned, Memphis turned to face the two ladies, clearly underwhelmed by their participation to date. "Well?"

Disappointed the shirt covered the nicest thing about the room, and feeling a little fuzzy, Kate murmured, "Nice. But I'll need to see the rest of them."

"Absolutely," the clerk said in agreement. "No need to be too hasty."

After several more rounds of the same, she and the clerk were no closer to choosing, and Kate was feeling even more light-headed as she drained the last of her wine. At this rate they could be here all day, and Memphis would have to cart her out of the private dressing room in a wheelbarrow.

Halfway through the shirt selections Memphis tried on one of his choices.

"How does that one feel?" Kate said.

He shrugged into the oxford. "Strangely enough," he said with a touch of sarcasm. "It feels like a shirt."

She rose from her seat, surprised to find her legs even more rubbery than they'd felt while sitting. Handing him the shirt with the higher thread count, she said, "Now try this."

Kate waited as calmly as she could as he slipped out of the first and into the second, pivoting to face the mirror.

She turned to inspect his reflection. "And?"

He cocked his head, meeting her gaze in the mirror. "I suppose if I have to attend this fancy freak show, I might as well be comfortable," he said. "This one is definitely softer."

A big I-won smile spread across her face. "I told you so."

His grin was deliciously tiny but big on meaning. "You're gloating."

"I'm just pleased that Memphis James can admit when he's wrong."

His voice lowered an octave. "Too bad Kate Anderson can't do the same."

She froze, staring at his reflection, wondering what, specifically, he was talking about. That she thought she'd been prepared for Memphis's presence in her life again? Or perhaps he was referring to her recent assessment of the night she'd made love to him, stating it had been a mistake? Or maybe her declaration she wouldn't repeat the same mistake again?

Feeling wobbly, Kate pivoted on her heel to face him, her back to the clerk, her voice low. "I'm not wrong."

"You are about several things."

The intense look on his face and the heat in his gaze seared her to the soul.

Seemingly oblivious to the tension, the clerk said, "If you don't mind me asking, Mr. James, how did you get those scars on your chest?"

Eyes on Kate, Memphis pulled off the shirt and handed it to her, a hint of humor in his gaze as he pointed to a small patch of purplish skin on his left side. "I got this as a teen when I tried a burn before I'd had any formal training." Memphis looked at the clerk and pointed to the well-healed, angry puckered line along his right collarbone. "Two years ago I took a fall and broke my clavicle. Despite the fracture, I did the stunt two more times to get the gag just right. By the time I was done the break was bad enough to require surgery."

And then his gaze switched back to Kate. "This last one is from a spill I took jumping my dirt bike six years ago," he said, pointing at the scar just below his navel, and the memory sent Kate's belly spiraling with all the stomach-dropping sensations of one of his high falls.

During the longest night of her life, she'd used her lips and tongue to trace the mark on his flat abdomen before moving lower. The wine was definitely having an effect now, because she was feeling decidedly unsteady.

From behind her, the clerk's voice sounded far away. "Shall I search for a few more items for you, Mr. James?"

Memphis's gaze bored relentlessly into Kate's, despite the fact he was addressing the redhead, his voice husky. "I have everything I need right here."

Kate's lips flattened and her chest pinched around her heart.

If the clerk was picking up on the undertones, hopefully she thought it was anger. Because Kate *was* angry, at Memphis for being so inappropriate and woefully unconcerned about their audience, and at herself—for still being susceptible to the bold, too-large-for-life Memphis.

Finally, the clerk said, "I'll be back in a few minutes to check on you."

His gaze shifted briefly to the woman. "I'd prefer that you didn't," he said, and Kate's belly burned at his frank words. His eyes returned to hers, and the tension in her insides reached levels that interfered with her ability to breathe as he went on. "Ms. Anderson and I will come find you when we're done."

A sensual heat and heart-thumping anticipation swelled so acutely it pushed the breath from her lungs and filled every available space in her stomach. As the salesclerk turned on her heel and exited, neither of them moved, their gazes engaged in a duel.

Once the lady pulled the door shut behind her, Kate took a deep breath and gathered her strung-out nerves, feeling woozy from the wine and the man. "Memphis, let's just concentrate on finishing."

He didn't move. "That's what I'm doing."

A crackling electricity hit her body and spread. "No, you're not," she said. "You're intentionally trying to make me uncomfortable. And that isn't going to help us complete our task," she said, and she turned to head for the rest of the shirts.

Memphis wrapped his fingers around her wrist, preventing her departure from his side, and her heart rate surged into overdrive as she reluctantly faced him.

His gaze was relentless. "Maybe that's not the task I'm trying to complete."

Oh, God. She wasn't ready for this.

She would *never* be ready for this.

Desperate to delay the inevitable, she said, "I don't know what you're talking about."

But she did, she just couldn't admit it, because right now his skin on hers reminded her of just how long it had been since she'd been touched by a man.

Fingers wrapped around her wrist, Memphis took a step closer. "Do you remember what you said the last time we made love that night?"

Kate's mouth went dry and her throat constricted, cutting off her breath. The heat of his palm was but a small reminder of the fire this man had the ability to create. It was several moments before she could answer. "No."

His eyes told her he knew she was lying. "You need a little more practice telling the truth, ex-Mrs. Worthington," he said, his deep voice rumbling up her spine. His tone was infused with the insatiable need they'd shared so long ago.

Along with a generous dose of frustration.

Memphis had always come with a tangle of emotions that had been impossible to unravel—some of them good, some of them bad, but none of them had been lukewarmly felt. Right now intense desire and a rising anger of her own was making rational thought difficult.

He was wrong for her. He'd *always* been wrong for her.

"Memphis," she said, struggling to stay calm despite the lack of oxygen. "I'm not—"

"You promised me the morning," he said smoothly.

Her heart tripped in her chest. "That was a long time ago." She pulled her hand free and took a step backward, trying to distance herself from the memories and all she'd done with this man, *to* this man, and the consequences. "And during a turbulent time in my life."

He went on as if she hadn't spoken, stepping forward in her direction even as she continued to back away. "And then I woke to find you gone."

Guilt, her ever-present companion, reared its persistent head.

"I was upset." She hated that her words came out weak. "And confused…"

As if that explained everything she'd done.

He continued to slowly advance on her as she backed up, until her shoulders hit the door and there was no more room for retreat. "There," he said softly, his gaze deliberately provoking her. "That will keep the overly helpful clerk out until we're through."

"We *are* through."

"Angel Face," he said, his voice gruff. "I've finally figured out we're so far from done it isn't funny."

Irritation drove her chin up. Memphis James might do what Memphis James wanted, but that didn't mean she had to be obliging. "There is nothing left—

He took her hand and placed her palm over the bared scar beneath his navel, and the tiny muscles in her fingers twitched, desire paralyzing the rest of her. Despite being no match for solid ground at high rates of speed, the heat and the hard planes of his abdomen were unyielding, as well.

"Do you remember kissing me here?" he said.

Her body flooded with fire. "Of course I do."

"Do you remember where your mouth went next?"

Her head swam with desire, and her protest came out as a weary groan. "Memphis—"

"Kate." He braced a hand on the door by her head, the other sandwiching hers against his taut abdomen. She could barely breathe, and the process grew more difficult as he leaned in until she could see the dark chocolate flecks in the caramel color of his eyes, smell the intoxicatingly masculine scent of sandalwood. "I want one more kiss."

And, as if knowing there'd be no consent, he simply took her mouth with his.

At the touch of his lips, it took every ounce of self-possession she could muster not to melt against him. The kiss wasn't gentle, but neither was it harsh, reflecting none of the frustration she sensed still simmered beneath his surface. Instead, there was a restrained curiosity in the way he moved against her. As if reacquainting himself with her texture, familiarizing himself with her flavor. Reexploring the depths of her mouth and just how deep their passion went.

She should push him away. Her conscience kept screaming there would be no redemption in seeking out the very man who knew just how far from perfect Kate Anderson had strayed. But it had been so long, and the cravings were so intense, that right now her body didn't care.

He pulled his head back a fraction, a faint

frown on his face, his eyebrows knitted together as if he was disturbed.

"Damn," he said, his voice disappointed. "You taste as good as I remember."

The second kiss was even harder to resist, and she relaxed a fraction as Memphis angled his head, firmly gathering her lips closer, taking the kiss so deep she began to lose hope she'd find her way back up. Their shared frustration finally made an appearance, too, along with an achy need so strong it rendered her helpless in her quest to push him away.

The pleasure pulsed higher, demanding to be recognized, and Kate knew her resistance was slipping away....

As their kiss continued Kate's mouth grew softer, and Memphis could feel himself grow harder, until desire firmly embedded itself in his body. He spent several seconds pressing his fingers into the door, trying to resist the alluringly sweet flavor with a hint of spice. Curiosity, the sense of challenge and a trace of irritation had brought about his actions. Resentment at being verbally dismissed by this woman who was so thoroughly a part of his past that he held few memories from his teens without her in them—the physical yearning, her cool treatment of him, her displeasure at his antics, his *character*. And then there was the pleasurable thrill at the rare appearance of the fiery Kate. All had combined to drive him insane.

But he'd only wanted one more kiss.

Unfortunately, now he knew the simple contact would never be enough.

And then Kate touched her tongue to his bottom lip, as if tentatively asking for more, and, with a groan born of years of living with the delicious memories, Memphis fisted his hand against the door and slanted his mouth across hers with a recklessness that probably wasn't wise. Drinking in the taste that had mesmerized him. The intoxicating mix of sweet submission and underlying strength of spirit that was singularly Kate.

Truth. It was all about *truth*.

For a brief moment Kate was admitting the attraction was still mutual, at least in body if not in words. It was the only time this woman, the one who had driven him mad in so many ways, was stripped of the hands-off aura she kept firmly in place.

As the seconds passed, need wove through his every cell, and he slid Kate's hand down his abdomen, over the denim of his jeans, and pressed her palm firmly against his erection.

An intense surge of pleasure shot through his body at the same time a tiny protest came from Kate's throat—a soft, barely heard noise that matched the free hand she used to press against his chest, and instinctively he knew what both actions meant.

Kate Anderson could kiss him as if he were the only man she'd ever wanted, even as she berated herself for her choice.

Memphis braced his fist against the door and pulled his mouth away. Heart pounding, he stared down at her flushed cheeks, the blue eyes now clouded with desire and the delectably parted lips, damp from his. Toss in the furrow of concern on her brow and it was more than any man should be forced to endure.

"Time for you to go, Kate," he said, his tone carefully even despite the heart pounding violently in his chest. "The clerk and I can take it from here."

CHAPTER FOUR

Two days later Memphis stared at the cloudless sky that domed over the Atlantic, the aquamarine color broken by the pier jutting into its waters. The dock contained the pyrotechnic crew and was littered with barrels, crates and fake cans of fuel. A fishing boat was moored at the end. Multiple cameras were set up to record the stunt from different angles.

Memphis adjusted the snatch harness hidden beneath his protective attire, the harness attached via a ratchet line to a heavy-duty hoist. Two propane-filled canisters were pointed directly at Memphis, the tanks set to detonate and shoot a blast of fire at the same time the hoist was to jerk him back, as if the explosion was knocking him into the water.

Memphis had been rehearsing this gag for days, connecting the various pieces of equipment and working on assuming a natural position in the air. He was good to go. Unfortunately, the crew wasn't ready, which meant Memphis was left waiting with too much time to think. Which was never ideal leading up to a particularly tricky stunt, but was particularly troublesome when he was stewing over problems unrelated to the task at hand, threatening his usual focus.

Bad things happened when his focus was off.

It had been forty-eight hours since he'd sent Kate from the designer store and finished the shopping. Despite her original insistence on being present for the selections, Kate had willingly bolted. Frustration welled again, and Memphis raked a hand through his hair, blowing out a long breath as he fought to control the sense of dissatisfaction.

Used to be, he'd been confident that when Kate grew up and stopped blindly following the wishes of her family, had stopped being the dutiful Anderson daughter long enough to stand up for what she wanted, then she would want *him* as much as he wanted *her*. After yesterday he wasn't so sure.

A faint frown crossed his lips. Maybe he'd read too much into the surreptitious glances he'd caught from her during their teens. Perhaps they'd been a figment of his overly hormonal imagination, and she hadn't been as attracted to him as he'd thought. The chemistry crackling between them could have simply arisen from the anger she felt as she repeatedly tried to get him and Brian to stop taking risks that got them into trouble—upsetting the image of the powerful Anderson family.

And maybe the night she'd spent in his arms

had simply been fueled by sorrow over the argument she'd had with her husband. Or maybe it was an attempt to get back at Dalton for his treatment of her. But even as the thought entered his mind, he knew it wasn't true. Kate Anderson might be a lot of things but she was neither vindictive nor cruel. No, the likely reason was far worse.

She might be attracted, but not enough for Memphis James to be worthy of a second look.

His lips twisted wryly at the bitter taste in his mouth. Being relegated to the insignificant defined the early years he'd spent living on the wrong side of the tracks, and was something Memphis had set about to change. He'd accepted being poor.

He'd refused to accept being treated as if he were invisible.

Immediately he was back ten years in time to being Tiffany Bettingfield's date to Kate and Brian's senior prom. Tiffany was just one of several girls at the private school who had asked him to attend. He'd had no interest in the lavish event, but couldn't resist the chance to see Kate in action—the biggest, most beautiful fish in her tiny pretentious pond. Their two-year age difference had seemed huge back then, and he'd been frustrated by his inability to let his fascination go. He *should* have been concentrating on the older females who had made themselves so available.

No doubt his friends would have been surprised by his choice.

But no one had been surprised when Kate was crowned Prom Queen next to her equally perfect Prom King, the man she'd eventually marry. When Memphis had approached them to offer his congratulations, simply a lame attempt to get her reaction to his invasion of her bright, shiny world, it was Dalton who'd been friendly, graciously shaking his hand. The blank look on Kate's face had left Memphis stewing. And then she'd sent him a cool smile and a polite nod, looking right through him before she turned to address a classmate.

He and Brian had achieved legendary status at the private school, a certain popularity with most of the students; but to Kate Anderson, Memphis was too insignificant for a short conversation. Worse, he couldn't shake his interest in the younger girl.

"Hey, Memphis," a familiar voice called, interrupting the disturbing memories, and Memphis turned and spied Kate's brother.

Tall and lean, Brian Anderson shared the same aristocratic features and blue eyes as his twin sister. In khakis and a T-shirt, the sandy-haired man made his way up the dock, heading for Memphis. His progress was marked with an uneven gait, favoring the leg that had been shattered in that fateful jump five years ago, and Memphis tensed.

Damn. Why had he come back to his hometown?

"Dude, you've been in Miami for...what, three weeks?" Brian said as he drew closer. "What took you so long to call and invite me down to see you in action?"

The guilt climbed higher. "Sorry, Brian," he said. "Last night was the first chance I got."

"Kate said she told you to call me," his friend said.

Memphis's lips quirked. Brian's sister was wrong about a lot of things, but she was right about him needing to call Brian. It had been way too long.

"How about we grab a beer tonight?" Brian said. "On a bar overlooking the beach, of course." Hair ruffling in the breeze, Brian shot Memphis that devil-may-care grin that was famous around Miami, his antics, paired with the prestigious family name, landing him in many a newspaper over the years. "It's good to see you, Memphis," he said, clapping him on the shoulder.

"You, too," Memphis said, and he meant it.

Brian nodded at the propane tanks. "Reminds me of when we first met," he said. "I was riding my dirt bike out at that old grove when I got splattered with a rotten orange you shot from your potato gun," he said as he sent Memphis a huge grin.

His mouth twisted in humor. "I told you," Memphis said. "That was an accident. Besides, I let you help me detonate those propane cylinders to make up for the hit." Memphis shot him a smile. "Suckers blew sky-high."

"And my heart didn't restart for a week."

"We were just lucky the orange grove didn't catch fire."

"What's really amazing is that we still have our hearing." The twinkle in Brian's eyes grew brighter. "If we had been smarter we would have started with one canister instead of lighting all three at once."

"Well," Memphis said with a laugh. "No one ever accused us of being smart."

Brian's laughter joined his and, for a few seconds, Memphis enjoyed the moment that was full of every stunt they'd pulled, starting out amateur and becoming more sophisticated over time. Some had been lame, some had been brilliant, but all of them had been born out of passion and forged in a kindred spirit that Memphis hadn't quite matched since.

Once the laughter died there was an awkward pause, and Memphis searched for a way to fill the blank. "How's work?" It was a stupid question, because Memphis had followed Brian's growing reputation as stunt coordinator on a local TV show that was garnering national acclaim. It was a double-edged sword. Memphis was enormously pleased with his friend's success, yet disturbed by the thought of what Brian could have accomplished without the injury bestowed upon him, courtesy of Memphis. With effort, he pushed the guilt aside as Brian went on.

"Work is good," Brian said. "Speaking of, I have a jump I'd like to discuss with you tonight." He shaded his eyes from the sun with his hand.

"And the beer is on me, as a thanks for helping Kate."

Instead of a painful groan, Memphis let out a noncommittal "Hunh" and paused to gaze out over the aquamarine waters of the Atlantic. The bright sun rippled on the water as he reined in the conflicting emotions.

"The divorce has been rough on her," Brian said. "I know in the past you two were always arguing, but try to be nice, okay?"

Clamping back the bark of an ironic scoff, Memphis was inordinately grateful when the crew signaled they were almost ready to start.

Memphis shot his friend a look. "Nice isn't my specialty," he said. "But I'll do my best."

The flash of fire was larger than Kate had expected, and the cable snatched Memphis up and back with a heart-stopping force. Her chest froze, refusing to cooperate with the act of breathing as Memphis arced through the air, his body assuming a ragdoll position that mimicked death. At least she hoped it was an act. If it wasn't, she was going to kill him herself for shaving five more years from her life.

Right after she'd set him straight about their kiss, of course.

Memphis hit the sun-dappled water, but Kate didn't breathe until his head popped above the surface. She gripped the barricade, steadying her annoyingly wobbly knees while she inhaled swiftly as the crew whooped and hollered their approval. The cheering continued until he climbed the ladder out of the water and appeared on the dock. Several of the staff surrounded Memphis to help unhook the cable and remove the harness strapped to his chest, and Memphis pulled off his wet shirt to wipe his dripping face.

Now free, a bare-chested Memphis made his way to the monitor where a few of the staff were gathered, as well as her brother. At the sight of the two men together again, her heart twisted nostalgically, but Memphis's attention was fully focused on the screen as the group watched the explosion and his flight from every camera angle. Kate studied his profile, fascinated by the concentration on his face as he reviewed the stunt he'd just performed. After a short discussion, the group disbanded and, with a nod at Memphis, her brother took off. Memphis headed for a portable canopy set up to provide escape from the sun, shading several card tables dotted with equipment. He was alone, so it was now or never.

And never was sounding pretty good.

Heart still thumping, she pushed aside the nervousness and rounded the barricade, targeting Memphis. When one of the crew noticed her, she braced, certain he'd tell her to get back behind the barrier. Instead, he nodded as she passed and greeted her with a "Mornin' Ms. Anderson."

Apparently Memphis had prepared the crew for the possibility of her appearance. As if he *knew* she'd come to discuss her participation in that kiss. Suddenly flustered, Kate checked her forward progress, her footsteps faltering as a rush of heated memory deep-fried her nerves. She longed for relief, but short of jumping into the blue waters of the Atlantic, that was a laughable goal, because Memphis's beautifully exposed torso was almost as good from the side view as the front.

At this rate, she'd need to carry a spare shirt for the man, just for such emergencies.

Memphis leaned over to examine a laptop computer, well-worn jeans slung low on his hips. The only thing sexier than Memphis James shirtless and in snug, faded jeans, was a *wet* Memphis in said condition. And the sight of his muscular thighs covered in naturally distressed denim was distressing her, as well.

Nerves vibrating with awareness, she approached him anyway. "How was the take?"

He cast her a glance from the corner of his eye. "It was a good shot," he said, not sounding surprised to see her. Clearly he'd been aware of her presence for a while.

"And if it hadn't been?" she said.

"I'd do the stunt again," Memphis said as he turned and met her face-to-face.

His wet hair looked darker, curling at the edges and exposing a cut on his forehead. Blood blended with the water dripping down his temple.

Concern drove her footsteps closer. "You're hurt."

Memphis wiped his forehead and looked surprised to find his fingertips tinged red. "Just a scrape."

"But you're bleeding," she said, and frustration over his nonchalant attitude pushed aside the last of her uncertainty and drove her forward until she stood in front of him.

Awareness lit his eyes, but his tone was dry. "I wouldn't come any closer," he said, nodding down at her summer pantsuit. "I might get you dirty," he murmured.

Simple, chic and made of the lightest of fabrics, the suit's minimalist look was one she loved and the delicate, dove-gray coloring was purely feminine. With a pair of high heels, she felt confident and ready for anything...except for the lightly mocking look from Memphis.

She took a steadying breath, catching the scent of salty sea mixed with hot, potent male, forcing her gaze to remain on his face. Unfortunately her peripheral vision was working well, and it was hard to ignore the wet chest and hard plane of muscle that were begging for the full attention of her eyes.

"Why are you here, Kate?"

The rough timbre of his voice set her pulse thumping.

"I came to remind you about tomorrow night," she said.

His lips curled at one end. "No you didn't."

His insistence on always calling her out left her irritated.

"I think I know the reason why I'm here," she

said as smoothly as she could. He might not care about polite protocol, but she did.

"You could have just called," he said. "Or texted me."

"I..." Her voice died, because she couldn't come up with a good excuse on such short notice. "I wanted to discuss how we'd ride to the dinner. And since I was passing by—"

He let out a bark of laughter. "You weren't passing by."

Kate curled her fingers against her palm. Simple small talk and graceful manners were outside the scope of the infuriating man's capability. Memphis did whatever Memphis wished and, unfortunately, denying her a graceful entrance into this discussion was on his agenda for today.

As if trying to explain the dressing-room fiasco wasn't difficult enough.

Buying time for composure, she nodded at the laptop computer, the screen containing a complicated mathematical equation. "What's that?"

"A stunt Brian and I were discussing."

"The dynamic duo is back at it again?" She could tell it was a bad choice for a question, his face remaining impassive, and she looked away, training her focus on the calculations on the computer. "What kind of math is that?"

"Trigonometry," Memphis said.

"And here I thought you were just another pretty face." And more than an eye could stand as drops of water beaded on the ripples of his chest.

"That's because you refused to see more,"

Memphis said with a sardonic tone. "If I want to determine the path my dirt bike will make when it hits a ramp at high rates of speed, trigonometry is necessary."

Her voice held more than a hint of shock. "You do calculations before your jumps?"

"Always. Even as a teen."

Surprise left her blinking hard as she remembered the many stunts she'd witnessed herself. A brazen adolescent Memphis, hot, sweaty and covered in dust. And Kate, her body on fire and her heart in her throat as he rode his dirt bike off a ramp. "I always assumed you were just winging it."

"I'm not surprised," he said. Although the familiar teasing smile was firmly in place, there was an underlying edge to his tone. "You assumed a lot of things."

Gazes locked, a wave of awareness moved through her. Not the sexual kind, that was permanently seared into her brain, thank you very much. No, this was an awareness of just how deep his anger went over her past treatment of him. She knew she deserved quite a bit of his bitterness. She also knew her cool treatment of him had been purely a defense mechanism, but she would never share that truth. Not when it could, and *would,* be used as ammunition against her.

A trickle of blood from his forehead merged with a salt-water drip from his hair, the bloody rivulet running down his temple.

Kate shifted on her feet. "At least let me clean up your cut."

Memphis heaved out a sigh, as if her response wasn't the one he'd been hoping for. Without a word, he rummaged through a plastic tote and pulled out a flat metal box, tossing the first-aid kit onto the table. "God forbid I stand between Kate Anderson and her attempt to keep the world neat and tidy, with everyone in their place."

Ignoring his words, Kate cleared her throat and opened the first-aid kit, hoping to change the conversation. "What time will you pick me up for the dinner party tomorrow?"

"Seven o'clock," he said as he sat in a folding chair.

She rummaged through the contents of the kit, the silence stretching between them. After gathering the necessary items, she rounded the table and stopped in front of Memphis.

"There are latex gloves in the box," he said, his dark gaze challenging hers. "So you don't have to get your hands dirty."

She paused, gauze in hand, and stared down into the decadent caramel eyes framed with water-spiked lashes, the sensual lips framed in half a day's stubble. The memory of her hand pressed against his erection in the dressing room resurfaced, heat surging in response. Kate blinked hard and bit the inside of her cheek, concentrating on the abrasion as she dabbed the cut to absorb the blood.

Kissing him might be out, but she definitely owed him an apology.

"I never thought you were dirty, Memphis," she said, carefully avoiding his gaze. "You were just...too much for me as a teen."

"Yeah," Memphis said slowly, staring up at her as her heart did a little twist. "I remember."

Unfortunately, so did she. Once, at sixteen, she'd hunted down her brother to warn him of their father's anger over Brian's latest escapade with Memphis. She'd found the two boys setting up a stunt, and Memphis had laughed at her concern, calling her Angel Face for the very first time. It was one of those few moments she'd lost her cool, and when Brian took off for the ramp on his dirt bike, she'd lit into Memphis. But her angry words had only made him smile bigger, and when she'd finished her tirade, he leaned in and kissed her.

Confused and so turned on her teenage body didn't know which way to turn, she'd slapped him in the face. One week later she'd started dating Dalton. Handsome, smart and easygoing, he was well loved by her parents. With the added bonus of not driving her crazy.

Memphis tipped his head. "That was a heck of a slap you gave me. But I was truly in awe of your ability to ignore the obvious."

Needing a moment, she averted her gaze, tossing the bloody gauze aside. As the silence ticked by between them, she searched for the cotton balls and the alcohol, her fingers clumsy. She could feel his expectant gaze. When she was finally steady enough to face him again, the rich caramel eyes with a hint of heat nearly stalled her heart. He was waiting for her to respond.

And she knew why.

"I..." Despite her attempt to keep her tone light, her voice faltered. "I shouldn't have kissed you back yesterday."

"Why not?" Memphis asked. "It's not like you're married anymore."

"But still," she said, dipping the cotton ball in the alcohol. "It was wrong and I apologize."

Memphis's hand shot up and wrapped around her arm, the cotton ball reeking of alcohol as she stared at him, heart pounding in her chest.

"It wasn't wrong, Kate," he said, his gaze intense on hers from below.

Fingers clamped around the soft cotton, she pulled her arm away. "I was drunk."

"You were tipsy."

"I was intoxicated," she said through clenched teeth.

"You had full command of your faculties and picture-perfect Angel Face doesn't want to admit it."

"And you're going out of your way to make this apology difficult," she said, and, with no gentleness in her touch, she plopped the alcohol-soaked swab directly onto the cut.

The swift intake of his breath was sharp. "That's because I don't want another damn apology," Memphis said, his voice hard. "I just want the truth."

They locked gazes and several seconds passed while Kate's heart struck her rib cage with added force. Now was the time to redraw the line in the sand. "There's only one truth, Memphis," she said. Finishing her task, she reached for the bandage, tearing open the package, her fingers clumsy. "We are not involved. We are just friends who made a mistake in the past."

Memphis hiked a brow skeptically. "Friends?"

Kate pressed her lips together, fighting the urge to let loose. But a verbal tirade, no matter how much Memphis James the Provoker deserved it, wouldn't help. She centered the bandage over his cut and smoothed the edges in place. "In a loose interpretation of the word, yes," she said. "Just friends." When he didn't respond, she brushed a stray strand of hair back from her cheek. "So, in keeping with our established relationship, I expect you to keep your hands to yourself at the dinner party tomorrow."

His chuckle came out as a throaty rumble that shimmied down her spine and spread outward, heating various parts of her body she'd have preferred to remain cold.

"When have I ever done what's expected of me?" he said.

Heart knocking harder, she blew out a long, slow breath. "Never," she said as coolly as she could, her tone firm. "But I'm looking forward to being pleasantly surprised."

His lopsided grin was enough to make a grown woman weep. "And I'm looking forward to disappointing you, Kate."

"Memphis." A tight smile plastered on her face, Kate gazed out the glass wall of the revolving restaurant overlooking the nighttime lights of downtown Miami. "Your hand on my back isn't exactly projecting the platonic attitude I was hoping for."

Not to mention the heat from his palm must surely be leaving an imprint on her now-sensitized skin. Not surprisingly, Memphis sounded unconcerned.

"My hand is a disappointing distance from your lovely breasts," he said. His sandalwood scent was especially distracting tonight. "And respectfully placed well above any other parts that could be considered sexual."

"It's too low," Kate said as quietly as she could given her irritation, praying the soft background music in the elegant bar covered their words. And, dear God, couldn't they shut down the revolving function of the top floor? Memphis's hand was making her dizzy enough. "Your fingers are too close to my backside. You need to shift your hand higher."

If for no other reason than to reestablish her ability to function, because her silk dress provided little protection from the commanding hand on her lower back. From the moment they had entered the room, his palm had settled in as if it owned the spot, and Kate's ability to make small talk had been sabotaged.

Which was a problem. Because her goal for tonight was to survive her first foray into the social world as a single woman with as much dignity and as few public ripples as possible. And that meant remaining cool and calm, an impossible battle with Memphis around. She'd barely made it through the introductions to the Robinsons, the couple hosting the evening. Not that introductions were necessary. Memphis's and Brian's notorious reputations had been well-known by her class in high school. Few had forgotten.

Nor had they forgotten her publicly scrutinized divorce.

Memphis splayed his fingers a little further, covering more of her back, and the unsteady feeling in her knees increased.

"Move. It. Higher," she said with false patience.

"Is there a minimum safe distance from your butt that I need to be aware of?" Memphis said dryly.

"Yes," she said. Anything that didn't leave her feeling so light-headed and turned-on.

He went on as if she hadn't spoken. "Because I can head back to my apartment and pick up my electronic tape measure that uses a laser to calculate distance."

The laser couldn't possibly sear her as thoroughly as his hand. "You don't need a ruler or any other measuring device. Just a sense of decency," she said as firmly as she could. "Right now your pinky is resting on my panty line."

"I was simply checking to see if you were wearing any," Memphis said, his voice easy, and then his little finger gently rubbed a small stretch of the elastic waistband of her undies.

She bit her lip, and then caught Susan Robinson looking at her strangely, so Kate worked hard at arranging her face into a pleasant expression. Unfortunately her muscles were so tense that pleasant and relaxed were next to impossible to achieve.

"And as far as I'm concerned," Memphis went on. "Touching a woman's back isn't considered a public display of affection. Unless, of course—" his voice grew deeper, and Kate knew she was in trouble "—I happened to be touching it with something other than my hand."

"Memphis," she groaned, half begging to spare her sanity and half reprimanding for the same reason. Her gaze landed on the waving figure of Cheryl Jackson, the woman making her way toward them with her husband in tow, and Kate lifted her hand in response, her smile now so rigid it could break glass from thirty paces away.

"I suppose there are several parts I could touch you with that would create a stir," Memphis said, amusement in his voice.

Heat flushed up her chest, her heart thudding as she forced herself to remain calm. Which was going remarkably well, considering.

Until the Jacksons drew closer, and Memphis

leaned in, his mouth just inches from her ear, his breath fanning across her neck. "Shall I try touching you with my tongue and see what kind of reaction we get from your old classmates?"

Kate swallowed hard and rallied her anger. She shot Memphis a look from the corner of her eye, hoping to silence the man who had apparently deemed it national Drive Kate Anderson Insane Day.

He was wearing a pair of dress pants he'd purchased that fateful day in the shop, along with a royal-blue tailored shirt that perfectly fitted his perfect chest. His angular jaw was clean-shaven, his light brown hair trimmed, but still with that slightly mussed look that gave him an I-just-crawled-out-of-bed air. Add to that his sinful eyes framed with long, dark lashes and the effect was one of overwhelming sex appeal that was impossible to ignore.

All of which was annoying, which meant the introductions were difficult when Cheryl and Ted Jackson stopped to say hello. Memphis's hand on her back was now so low two of his fingers lay south of her panty line. Kate was only too aware of exactly how big a mistake she'd made when she'd kissed him, and that Memphis had every intention of making her pay. She worked hard at forcing her face to relax as she chatted with the couple.

As the minutes passed, more committee members stopped to greet them. Which meant more introductions. And with every one of them,

Memphis was no help at all. And when the last couple moved on as the call to dinner was announced, Kate turned an exasperated fake smile on Memphis. "If you don't quit with the torture I'm going to test your high-fall skills by pushing you out that window."

Memphis tipped back his head and let out a laugh, his Adam's apple bobbing in delight. Even his neck looked strong, corded with sinew, and brought back memories of...

Enough.

The amused glimmer in his eyes was directed at her. "I'm just testing those political schmoozing skills you've acquired over the years."

"I've never had to be politely social while being manhandled."

"Doesn't speak much to the imagination of your ex," he said. "And Angel Face—" Memphis tipped his head "—if I was manhandling you, you'd know it." He paused before he went on, and the timbre of his voice dropped to a level that resonated low in her belly. "And knowing you the way I do," he said, his voice rough. "You'd probably enjoy it."

The unsteady sensation increased significantly and she blinked hard, trying to smooth the turbulent emotional eddies curling in her veins. A cool demeanor was impossible to maintain when the frustratingly contrary and rebel man was around.

"Memphis," she whispered fiercely, fighting for patience as she took a subtle step to the left, an unsuccessful attempt to remove her back from his touch. "This is difficult enough as it is. So keep your hand in a respectable place and stop trying to sabotage my attempts at being social."

The desperation in her tone must have pricked his interest. "Christ, Kate. Try to relax," he said, dropping his hand and tipping his head with a skeptical curiosity. "It's just a simple dinner. Why are you so uptight?"

"Maybe because this is my first social function since the divorce and I'm an object of scrutiny," she said. "Maybe because you are deliberately trying to make me uncomfortable." Frustration infused her tone as she shared more than she'd planned. "And maybe because I don't know how to behave."

He narrowed his eyes in confusion, and she went on with a sigh. "Technically, this is my first date."

His eyebrows puckered together. "I know, but it's just like riding a bike. It'll all come back to—"

"I've never been out on a date with anyone other than Dalton," she blurted, and immediately felt ridiculous.

Memphis stared at her, and with the inspection came an increasing flush of discomfort.

"Never?" he said, disbelief in his expression.

She blinked back the churning emotion and shook her head, turning her gaze to the window and concentrating on the incremental shift in the view of the lights of downtown Miami, the restaurant oh-so-slowly spinning on its axis. She could sense his gaze on her face and she closed her eyes. "Please stop staring at me as if I'm a freak."

"If I'd known how momentous this occasion was," he said. "I would have brought you flowers or something."

"It's not momentous," she said. "It's... It's..."

She was twenty-eight years old. It was embarrassing.

Humiliating.

"Awkward," she finally went on.

"Kate," he said softly, and she turned to look at him, seeing an expression of reassurance. "It'll be okay. You're doing great," he said soothingly, and he surprised her when he placed his hand between her shoulder blades. "Now let's just go enjoy our dinner."

CHAPTER FIVE

MAYBE he'd been too optimistic about enjoying dinner.

The food was delicious, each course more delicate and flavorful than the one before, but, as far as Memphis was concerned, it was a whole lot of trouble just for one meal. Because while the private dining room's view of the city slowly changed as the restaurant revolved, the view for Memphis was the same. The couple seated across the table were two of the most self-absorbed people he'd ever encountered. And the pair had no compunction about sharing their opinionated ideas, either.

"I'm so glad you came tonight," Tabitha Reed said to Kate, her green eyes sliding to Memphis, but he ignored the suggestive look.

"We didn't think you would after what your ex-husband just pulled," the lady's husband added. Blond and blue-eyed, Jim Reed sported classic good looks, an apparent indifference for his wife's wandering eye and a total lack of consideration for others. "Especially with the whole town talking about the scandal."

Kate sent the couple a polite smile they didn't deserve. "There *is* no scandal." Her tone was smooth, though Memphis sensed her discomfort. "The media just wants one in order to sell papers."

As usual Kate oozed class and a reserved charm as glossy as polished marble. Her simple rose-colored silk dress was elegant, and her wheat-colored hair was coiled at the back of her head, a style that left too much tempting skin of her graceful neck exposed.

"But your divorce wasn't final until three months ago," Tabitha said, either oblivious or not caring she was making Kate uncomfortable. "And Dalton is already engaged to another woman."

"We were separated several months before that," Kate said.

"Hon," Tabitha Reed said, brushing a chin-length strand of black hair from her cheek. "I don't know how you can defend him."

"I wish Dalton the best," Kate said, her expression coolly genuine.

Tabitha raised a skeptical brow.

"I truly do," Kate went on.

"Well," Tabitha said, picking up her drink. "I think you're way too forgiving."

Memphis agreed. The insensitivity of the woman was beginning to grate on his nerves.

And how could Kate calmly sit there and take all their bullshit?

"Did you see the picture that was just posted on the reunion website?" Tabitha said.

The woman's husband felt inclined to help out. "It's in the then-and-now section," he said. "A brilliant addition, by the way. Placing current photos of classmates juxtaposed to their high-school photos should help out at the reunion." Jim Reed went on, "I wouldn't recognize some of the people today."

"I know," his wife said, laying a hand on her husband's arm. She leaned in, addressing their little end-of-the-table foursome conspiratorially. "Did you see the photo of Virginia Torrington? I mean, really," she said, rolling her eyes. "As if she didn't go under the knife for that new nose."

Memphis had no idea who the lady was referring to, and he sure as heck didn't care. As far as he was concerned, dessert couldn't come fast enough.

"Great idea to get the website up, Kate," Jim said.

"Kate's done a wonderful job as chairperson," Tabitha Reed gushed, but it was the kind of enthusiasm that left one uneasy.

"Thank you," Kate said. "I've had a lot of help—"

"Memphis," Tabitha interrupted, turning to address him. "You should have seen the fundraiser Kate organized for Dalton last year. It was the talk of the town and well-attended. I don't think I've ever seen the reception hall at the Samba Hotel look so beautiful." The black-haired woman beamed her smile in Kate's direction. "Everything Kate touches turns to gold."

Kate's expression didn't change, but Memphis could feel the tension rolling off her now. It had started out as slight, but the longer they were held captive in this couple's conversation, the more strained her smile became. And the more he had trouble keeping his mouth shut.

"You're too kind," Kate said, her voice smooth.

Kind? Memphis shot Kate a questioning look, but she ignored him. There was nothing benevolent about Tabitha Reed. The smile on the woman's face didn't reflect the light in her eyes.

"Oh, please," Tabitha went on. "Everybody wanted to be Kate Anderson in high school. You were the most popular girl, you had a famous family *and* you dated Dalton." Tabitha's tiny laugh sounded forced. "I had such a crush on him back then. Even I was a little jealous of the girl who had everything."

And Memphis finally realized what this conversation was about, the subtext clicking into place. There was no well-meaning sympathy from this woman regarding Kate's recent difficulties, and Tabitha wasn't simply being an insensitive ass. Instead, she'd corralled Kate at the end of the dinner table with every intention of venting years of resentment and envy.

And Kate was politely going along with her

plans, but Memphis's patience was growing thinner by the second.

Even her husband was beginning to look uncomfortable. "The message board on the reunion website has been hopping with activity," Jim Reed said, as if trying to change the subject. "Based on the numbers so far, I bet we get better than a twenty-five-percent attendance."

"I know," Tabitha said. "Did you see the number of people that confirmed after Deena posted that wonderful picture of Kate and Dalton?"

Kate froze, and Memphis leaned in, prepared to tell the woman to go to hell.

But Kate laid a discreet hand on his knee, as if to hold him back. "What picture?" Kate asked.

"Your shining moment of course, silly. It's of you and Dalton being crowned at the Prom," Tabitha said, her smile too wide to be believed. "Isn't that ironic?"

A muscle in his jaw knotted as Memphis struggled to keep his mouth shut. He'd promised himself he'd try to make Kate's first date enjoyable. Cussing at their table companions probably wouldn't achieve the goal.

Kate's voice wasn't as strong as usual. "I didn't realize that had made its way onto the photo album."

"It was posted yesterday morning," Tabitha said. "And since then we've had a fifteen-percent hike in our attendance confirmations." The woman's bobbed black hair shifted forward as she leaned in, clearly excited. "It's fantastic news."

Fantastic.

As if Kate should be thrilled.

Memphis's patience ground to a complete halt. "Who knew a public divorce could come in so handy?" His voice was hard, his expression way too unforgiving to be mistaken for humor. Kate's fingernails gently bit into his knee, and she sent him a sideways glance intended to get him to hold his tongue. But he went on anyway. "Perhaps Kate should get married and divorced all over again. All in the name of a better attendance rate, of course."

"Memphis," Kate said, her voice strained.

But Memphis had had enough of her yielding to Tabitha's every malicious whim.

Kate straightened her shoulders and sent their table companion a gracious smile. "I'm simply pleased that—"

"The dinner was so delicious," Memphis finished for her as he stood. "Unfortunately, we have to go." His smile lacked even a hint of warmth. "I hope you enjoy your dessert."

Silently fuming, Kate didn't resist when Memphis held her elbow as he escorted her out of the crowded restaurant, the tension heavy between them. When they reached the empty bank of elevators, Memphis finally spoke.

"Damn it, Kate," he said. "What the hell was that all about?"

Kate pulled her arm from his grasp. "I'm the one who should be asking *you* that question."

Memphis ignored her response as he stabbed the down button for the elevator. "That woman maliciously droned on and on and you just rolled over and played dead."

"Listen, hot shot. Being confrontational doesn't make you brave. What purpose would it have served if I'd challenged her?"

"For starters it would have gotten her to shut up and leave you alone," he said as they entered the elevator. The door closed behind them, and he cocked his head, almost as if he was disappointed in her behavior. "And where was the spunky new Kate Anderson tonight?" he went on. "You know, the one with the backbone?"

Kate inhaled slowly, struggling to hold her temper. "Someone had to remain calm and rational. And as the former wife of a state representative, I'm accustomed to—"

"Is that all you've been doing these past few years?" He folded his arms across his chest. "Training to be nothing more than the well-behaved wife?"

"Dalton and I were a team, a team I *chose* to belong to."

His brow crinkled with impatience as he drawled, "You have a lot more to offer the world than simply being the senator's compliant daughter and the dutiful spouse of a state representative."

Irritation crept higher. "I played a part that I loved," she said. "Dalton might be one of the youngest representatives ever elected, but he is a brilliant politician, and I happen to know for a fact that he is committed to serving the people. His policies are ones that I care about, that I support. Which was why I volunteered to be in charge of his fundraising events."

"But all you accomplished was to further your *husband's* career."

Irritation gave way to anger, complete and absolute. "It might not mean much to you, Memphis," she snapped, stepping closer. "But I enjoyed what I did and I excelled at my job. Even with all of his faults, Dalton has *always* been more than generous in acknowledging my role in getting him elected."

Two seconds ticked by before he responded. "Of course he did," he said with a frustratingly calm tone. "Because you were supplying what he needed."

Kate pressed her lips together, staring Memphis down as the elevator door slid open, and then she turned and exited.

Still fuming, she didn't speak as the valet brought the car around, and she continued to stew on the drive home, furious at his words. And partially annoyed with herself. She knew most of the town thought the same thing, that there was little to Kate Anderson other than being Dalton's ex-wife.

And a tiny part of her wondered if it was true.

Good God, wasn't that a depressing thought? She closed her eyes, rubbing her forehead with her fingers.

"You okay?" Memphis said quietly, downshifting as he turned into Kate's neighborhood.

She stared out the passenger window and gave a small nod, dropping her hand to her lap as the streetlights streaked by in the night. As trial dates went, this one had been a disaster. And while she realized the circumstances were unusual, and Memphis was pure trouble, a part of her doubted that time and a different man would have made any difference. She was normally confident, more than able to hold her own during a lively debate with a room full of political powerhouses. But put her alone with a guy with romantic intentions and she suddenly was as uncomfortable as an awkward teen.

"You know," Memphis said, pulling her out of her thoughts. "You don't have to go to this reunion. I don't think anyone would fault you for skipping out."

She turned to look at him, studying the masculine profile of his face. "I want to go," she said firmly. Because it was the truth. "Organizing this event was the only pleasure I had these past months. And I'm not going to miss out on the fruits of my efforts just because of the Tabitha Reeds of the world."

Memphis looked at her, his voice rumbling with approval. "Good for you."

Her smile took on a self-deprecating touch. "I don't know if it's *good* for me, but I suppose it does make me out to be less of a coward," she said.

Guilt trickled across his face, and he returned his attention to the road that glowed in the light of the headlights. "You're not a coward."

"That's not what you just implied."

The lines of regret in his brow grew deeper. "I shouldn't have said that. How you deal with Tabitha is your business. And I shouldn't have given you a hard time about not wanting to go to these functions alone. I can see now just how difficult the situation is for you, and how—" He looked as if he was struggling for the right word. "How complex it is."

Complex? What an understatement. Especially given that the man she was taking to the events was the one guy she should be keeping her distance from.

She shoved away the thoughts and shifted in the seat to face him.

"It can't be easy to have people judging you and talking about you behind your back," he said.

She hiked a brow. "I wouldn't know. I'm too busy dealing with what they're saying to my face." He let out a soft laugh, the sound full of ironic amusement, and she went on. "I'm not concerned with what Tabitha Reed thinks, or doesn't think, about me."

"You shouldn't be. And…" he said, shoving a hand through his hair, "I've changed my mind about the reunion. If it will make it easier for you, I'll attend the second reunion event." Kate stared at him, but he kept his eyes on the road. "And while I'm apologizing," Memphis said, his voice turning rough. "I'm sorry I put down your role in your marriage. I shouldn't have implied what you were doing held no value. Clearly you deserve credit for your help in getting Dalton elected."

She blinked twice, trying to adjust to the turn of events before responding.

The rough-and-tumble, to-hell-with-the-rest-of-the-world Memphis James agreeing to attend both reunion events. And apologizing—minus the mocking tone.

It was hard to assimilate all at once, much less while she was feeling particularly vulnerable.

Don't go there, Kate.

She swallowed hard, hoping the large, rock-like object in her throat would prevent her from saying something stupid. "Thank you," she said softly, and then she turned to face forward, quitting while she was ahead. Before she spouted something really ridiculous, like *hold me*. She'd begged him to do that once before. How could she get her life back in order if she stepped in that mess again?

Memphis turned into her driveway, and she felt, rather than saw, his glance at her from the corner of his eye. "What are you thinking?" he said.

"I feel..." Kate stared at the three-story, Spanish-style home Dalton had given her in the divorce settlement. "I feel lost."

The tone of her voice must have disturbed Memphis, because he gripped the steering wheel hard as he parked the car in the driveway. "Hell,

Kate," he said softly, staring up at her house. "Who wouldn't feel lost in this monstrosity?"

They stepped out and closed the doors, and Kate rounded the front of the car, staring up at the house. "It is a little big."

Memphis joined her, resting his hip on the hood of his vehicle. "*Little* doesn't belong anywhere near a sentence describing this property."

Despite her best effort, a sliver of defensiveness crept into her voice. "We bought it because the formal living and dining area were perfect for entertaining," she said. "And the size was nice because it was convenient when Dalton's extended family came for a visit."

"Perfect for housing a small nation, too," Memphis said dryly.

"But too big for a divorced woman living alone."

An awkward silence fell between them, blanketing the mood with tension again. There was no relaxing with Memphis around, and after the evening she'd had, relaxation was definitely in order. But the thought of entering her house alone, left to rattle around until she finally fell into an exhausted sleep, held zero appeal. She'd done that too much lately.

She turned to look at him. "Is this the part where I'm supposed to ask you in for a drink?"

"Only if you want to be completely unoriginal."

She hiked a brow. "I think I've had enough originality for tonight." His eyes crinkled with amusement, at least until she went on. "So...will you come in?"

The humor in his gaze was slowly replaced with caution. "One drink and then I'll go."

Feeling like a gawky teen, body thrumming with the possibilities, Kate weighed his response as she led him up the walk and into the house, heading for her living-room bar. Despite the fact he'd stopped to lean against the doorjamb to the room, his presence seemed to fill the space, the fine physique, the bedroom eyes, the sexily mussed hair...

Unfortunately, the memories of making love to this man made her fingers clumsy, the glass rattling as she poured a brandy. Apparently Memphis sensed her inner turmoil.

"Kate," he said, hesitation in his expression. "Why am I here?"

For a long moment she fought the answer that formed, but it was no use. It had been years since that time he'd made her feel so alive. Despite the shame that had come with the event, despite the years of regret, she longed to recapture the little light that night had brought to her life.

Finally making the inevitable decision, the only decision she could, she set the bottle down and crossed the room, placing her hands on his chest. "I want you to stay the night, Memphis."

His caramel eyes took on the color of very dark chocolate. She held her breath, hoping he'd say yes. Praying he'd say no.

And wishing she wasn't living so close to the edge of insanity these days.

He stared down at her for a long, uncomfortable moment, his eyes full of doubt. His voice was gruff. "I'm not part of an escort service."

She closed her eyes, feeling unsure, but the heat and the muscle beneath her hand—and the memories—called to her. She lifted her lids, took his hand and pressed his palm to her breast.

Memphis froze, and then his jaw muscle twitched. "I'll admit you make a convincing argument," he said slowly, his voice full of tension. "But this wasn't part of our agreement."

"I'd like to amend the agreement."

"A deal is a deal."

"Deals can always be renegotiated."

Several seconds passed as his dark eyes searched hers, and then he said softly, "Why should I?"

Because Tabitha's mention of Kate's old perfect life still held her in its grips. Because she was tired of rattling around the house that represented a dream that had fallen apart. But mostly, it boiled down to the length of time since she'd been touched by a man. Had felt wanted. *Desired.* Memphis had always made her feel that way.

Even when it had been wrong.

"Because I want you to make love to me," she said.

Memphis's lips twisted wryly. Just a few days ago, her answer would have been enough, and the tempting curve of her breast beneath his hand was sending signals his body insisted he not ignore.

When it came to Kate he had no shortage of desire. But as he learned more about her current situation, there was also a growing awareness of her vulnerabilities. Even though he'd promised himself never to feel sorry for this woman again, tonight had changed his mind. Though frustrating, her graceful dignity under fire was admirable. And when she had stared up at this big house, the lost look on her face had nearly done him in.

Lust alone was fine. But lust mixed with sympathy was dangerous.

"I think I should go," he finally said.

"I want you to stay."

Damn, he shouldn't need her to push him away.

Torn, he looked around her living room and the foyer—a sea of off-white stucco, wrought-iron fixtures and hardwood floors—his every nerve aching to take her. Unfortunately everything about Kate was complicated. Their rocky relationship. Their difficult, turbulent past.

His conflicting feelings...

His doubtful look was probably bigger than it should have been. "Kate, it's a bad idea—"

She rose on tiptoe and placed her mouth on his, stunning him with her actions. For five pounding heartbeats filled with her enticing scent, he battled the need.

And then he gripped her shoulders with the

vague thought of pushing her away. But her mouth moved against his with an allure that allowed little room for rational thought, and he was left halfheartedly maintaining their distance. Not pushing her back, as he knew he should, yet not pulling her closer, either, as he wanted to do. Instead, he remained frozen, enjoying her passionate plea even as his brain insisted he'd regret it in the end.

Kate softly nipped his lower lip, and, with a groan that took place in his mind only, Memphis tipped his head to the side, succumbing to the overpowering need to take more. He dipped his tongue against hers. She smelled sweet and tasted even sweeter, pure deliciousness wrapped up in a delicate female softness, yet coated with a hint of abandon.

The pleasurable torture continued with a mix of lips and tongues and lust, until he remembered that morning all those years ago—waking to find her gone—and his hands on her arms began to push her away.

Mouth fused with his, Kate clutched his shirt with frantic fingers, pushing him back toward the base of the staircase until he thumped against the wall, driving his need higher. It was almost as though she was afraid he would escape.

And maybe that was what this was all about. A chance for her to forget. To bury her head and ignore her problems, the way she always did. He frowned even as he continued to enjoy her soft lips, the sensual slide of tongue against tongue.

The sweet taste of citrus and the smell of lavender invaded his system and made resistance difficult.

He tried anyway. Because he needed a moment to think. Time to breathe. Memphis pulled his lips back a fraction. "Angel Face, you need to slow down—"

"No." Her mouth landed back on his as her fingers began to fumble with his buttons.

Desire battered him, growing stronger as the memory of their first time together came roaring back. She'd been as needy and out of control then as she was now. That night it was the shaking fingers, the hesitant uncertainty and the sweetness beneath her desperately bold maneuvers that had finally banished his thoughts of waiting until she was less emotional.

But this time, the sweet submissive side was nowhere to be found.

Kate wrestled with the front of his shirt until the top button popped, landing on the hardwood floor with a soft click.

He lifted his mouth a fraction. "Shouldn't that have held together better, given how much I paid for it?" he said.

"Probably," she said distractedly, her fingers still working, and a second button hit the floor.

Memphis didn't give a damn about the clothes, but his tenuous control on his sanity was close to shattering. Especially as she fought to finish the buttons. "You're ruining my shirt," he said.

Fingers gripped on the front of the garment, blue eyes smoldering, Kate took several backward steps up the stairs, pulling him along with her, her hot gaze now level with his. Turning him on as never before.

"I'll buy you another one," Kate said.

"I went through a lot to find this one," he said gruffly as he trailed behind her.

Now a quarter of the way up the grand staircase, Kate pulled his shirt off, tossing it aside, and it landed on the banister, draping across the handrail like a banner. "I'll help you pick out another," she said, and then threaded her fingers through his hair and pulled his head in the direction of hers.

"Damn it, Kate," he muttered just before he gave in to another soul-drugging kiss that snapped a few more threads of his control.

He gripped the dress covering her thighs, bunching the silk as he fisted his hands. After allowing himself a moment to slant his mouth across hers, to lose himself in another taste, he finally managed to regain a semblance of restraint and pulled his mouth away.

"I don't have a condom," he said.

Showing no mercy, Kate unfastened his belt, removed it and tossed it aside. "It doesn't matter. I'm on the Pill."

He scowled skeptically. "How do you know I don't have anything catching?"

"Do you?"

"No," he said, his scowl growing bigger. "But you don't know that."

Fingers through his belt loops, eyes on fire, she pulled him up several more steps. "I trust you."

They spent several minutes making their way higher in a give-and-take battle for the lead, Kate urging him up the stairs even as Memphis attempted to slow the progression by occasionally pinning her against the wall—a lame attempt to buy himself time to regain control. Lame because each time he caved in to his cravings, taking her mouth with his, the kisses grew rougher. Caught between his need to resist the hold the memories had over him even as he longed to give in.

They reached the last step before the landing, and Kate unfastened his pants and pushed them to the floor with a thunk, her hands greedy as they skimmed across his chest, lighting him on fire.

At this rate, he was going to be finished before he'd even mentally committed to participating.

"Kate, I think—"

She pressed him back again and this time his shoulder bumped a picture on the wall, knocking the frame to the stairs several steps below where it shattered with a crash.

But Kate, fastidious, painstakingly correct Kate, didn't notice.

And Memphis's reluctant mind finally fully aligned itself with the rest of his body. With a curse, he released the longing and frustration and the acute ache, cupping her buttocks and pulling her closer. He lifted her until his brief-covered erection nestled between her legs, consuming her mouth in an act of ownership that was as much about his own capitulation as it was about his possession of Kate.

Mind spinning, he finally allowed himself to indulge in his craving for the feisty woman he'd pushed so hard to uncover. All his teasing looks and goading words, taking delight when the real Kate would emerge, briefly dropping the ice-princess facade in exchange for the fiery girl/woman who had lit his adolescent years and set him ablaze. And for the first time she was taking what she wanted, even if it was only physically. It was intoxicatingly sexy, this irresistibly full-blooded Kate he'd waited so long to see. Asserting herself. Making her wishes known and not taking no for an answer.

He'd wanted her to do as much at dinner.

He'd settle for now.

Lips consuming hers, relishing the seductive rasp of tongue against tongue, he pulled the pins from her hair, freeing the silken strands as he backed her toward the first closed door he saw, his heart pounding with the need to be inside this woman.

When he pinned her against the bedroom door, Kate pulled her mouth from his. "Wrong room," she said.

"What the hell difference does it make?"

"I want you in *my* room."

Frustrated, Memphis rolled until his back was against the wall, freeing Kate from the pinned position. He gripped the hem of her dress, hauled it over her head and gave it a careless toss. The red silk sailed over the railing overlooking the foyer, fluttering out of sight to the floor below.

Arms wrapped around her, he kissed her with the same urgency that raged in his veins, working to release her bra as he steered her backward down the hall for the next room. When he pushed her against the second door, he let out a sigh of relief as he dragged her bra off and tossed it over his shoulder.

"This isn't the right room, either," Kate said.

Need now at a critical level, Memphis muttered, "Damn it, Kate." He reached for her hips and pulled her against him, arching his hard body against the enticing softness of hers. "Where's your bedroom?"

"Third floor."

He eyed the spiral staircase at the end of the long hall. Knowing death by explosion was imminent if he didn't have this woman soon, he realized he had to take matters more firmly in hand.

Not bothering with a warning, Memphis leaned down and hoisted Kate over his shoulder.

CHAPTER SIX

"MEMPHIS," Kate choked out, closing her eyes, breathless from desire and the awkward position. Being hauled like a sack of flour was hardly the romantic ending she'd envisioned as she'd all but dragged him up the stairs. "Wait—" She opened her eyes, and the sight cut off her protests.

The upside-down view of Memphis's backside could only have been improved with the loss of the white briefs that stretched across his tight rear end. Mesmerized, Kate watched the alternating bulge and lengthening of the corded muscles of his buttocks and thighs as Memphis carried her with impressive speed up the spiral staircase to the eagle's-nest guest suite. The space had been her bedroom since the end of her marriage.

Dizzy with desire, hot blood surging through her veins, she fought for breath as he mounted the last step, crossed into the suite and set her down in the middle of the room.

She didn't want to miss a thing, so she pushed the hair from her eyes, and was a little disappointed he didn't instantly pick up where they'd left off. Instead, as if stunned, he looked around at the slate-blue walls, the feminine Battenberg lace curtains and matching bedspread—covered in every outfit she'd nervously tried on and dismissed before tonight's dinner.

Memphis's gaze was firmly fixed on the queen-size bed, clearly meant for one.

Heat flushed up her neck, and she felt a sudden need to explain. "Before Dalton and I officially separated, I moved out of our master bedroom."

"How long ago was that?"

She hesitated for several heartbeats. "Eighteen months."

A stunned silence followed and his brows reached for the ceiling. "You're kidding me."

A twinge of self-consciousness twisted in her chest. "By the time we'd finally accepted the fact that our marriage was over, it was only six months before the election."

Memphis stared at her skeptically. "What did that have to do with anything?"

The twinge in her chest grew stronger. "I told you, I believe in Dalton's policies," she said, knowing the excuse sounded inadequate. "And I loved being the driving force behind his fundraising events."

She didn't add that her role had given her a sense of fulfillment she'd desperately needed. Or that it had seemed logical at the time. But now she wondered if there weren't bigger issues at hand. Namely, a fear of being alone.

Memphis's silence made her uncomfortable,

and she felt the need to fill it. "I was the one to suggest we maintain appearances until the election was over and things had time to settle."

His expression remained incredulous. "Was it your idea to be locked in a chastity tower?"

"It was of my own making."

"No men have been up here since you two decided to separate?"

"Not unless you count Frank who did the remodeling." Despite the fact that Memphis wore nothing but tight briefs, and his finely honed torso made conversation difficult, she said, "And even though it's been two years since I've had sex, I'm not into seventy-year-old men."

"Two years," he said, as if still struggling to take it all in. And then his attitude gradually shifted, his eyes growing dark as he slowly came toward her, his rumbling words loaded with meaning. "So what are you into, Kate?"

His predatory look was mesmerizing, and the rate of her breathing increased as she struggled for an answer to the delicately worded question about her sex life. She lifted her chin in defense of her choices. "Solitary activities."

As he came closer, a second emotion briefly flashed across his face, a cross between a disturbed-by-her-choices look and sympathy-for-the-reasons expression.

But she'd had enough pity these past few months to last her lifetime. "You can make it up to me."

Instantly the last trace of sympathy disappeared and his demeanor returned to one of pure predator. "How?" he asked, and then he shed his underwear and she bit her lip at the raw glory, the pure masculine form primed and intent on her.

Her voice was husky. "That was a good start."

"I'm thinking I need a few more details," he said, his hot gaze intense as he took the last step separating them, the long, lean, wonderfully muscled body so close she could feel his heat. "What else does Kate Anderson want?"

"For you to make love to me in every room of this house?" An embarrassing amount of hope radiated in her tone.

"I'm in good shape—" He leaned in for a kiss that sent her spiraling, his tongue taking a quick taste of hers before he pulled his head back. "But I don't think even my stamina is up to that kind of endurance test."

She wrapped her arms around his neck, desperate to keep him close. "It's been so long I might finish before you get started," she said, hoping he'd take the hint.

Without a word, not bothering with the bed covered in clothes, Memphis dragged her down to the thick carpet as he threaded his fingers into her hair, tilting her head so he could take her mouth again. And, this time, the intent behind it was clear. The fusion of lips and heat and tongue held a determined quality that made it clear that Memphis wasn't going to stop until he was through. Kate nearly cried in relief. Mouth on hers, he skimmed one hand down to stroke her skin, caress a breast, lingering a moment to tease the tip until she was ablaze.

And then his hand began to drift lower.

But she burned for more than just his fingers. "I want—"

As expected, the first second he touched her between the legs, pleasure flared. She instinctively arched, allowing him better access. The following second, his fingers skillfully began to tease her into wanting more. Which was hysterical, not to mention totally unnecessary, because on the third second she came.

With a burst of bottle rockets, fiery sparkles of heat shot to every corner of her body, leaving little sizzles fizzling in their wake, her limbs warm and heavy and limp.

Heart pounding, soul singing, she closed her eyes and whispered, "I told you."

"It might have something to do with the months trying to make do in sexual solitary confinement."

Talk was the last thing on her mind, especially this discussion.

Several moments passed before Memphis spoke again. "Kate," he murmured. When she lifted her lids, his gaze was close. "Did you think about our time together during those nights you spent satisfying yourself?"

"Sometimes," she said.

Always.

His eyes were a disturbingly burn-the-roof-of-your-mouth melted caramel. "Show me."

Her mind balked. "I can't—"

Memphis took her hand and slid it down between her legs. Fingers pressed over hers, he began to apply the same skill as before, but it was difficult to tell where she began and he ended. Warmth swamped her body and moisture flooded her center as the pleasure climbed higher, until her body screamed for a more satisfying contact.

"Memphis," she said, her voice breathless. "Don't make me wait any longer."

Elbow propped on the floor beside her head, their laced fingers caressing her clitoris, Memphis thrust deep between her legs.

The sensation was profound, much more than physical. For the first time in she couldn't remember when, she didn't feel so alone. This man knew her better than anyone—even those she loved the most.

Their entwined fingers and locked hips began to move together, establishing an agonizingly sensual rhythm. It was impossible not to drift between the delicious memory of their night long ago, the months of fantasies and the even better here and now—his hard body, the firm plane of chest muscles shifting beautifully with his efforts. Their contact limited to their laced fingers and their rocking hips, the coordinated movements created an intensity that was clearly meant as an attempt to compensate for all the nights she'd spent trying to get by alone.

In the end he might have wanted to draw it out, to take it slow and allow her time to savor the moment. Whether it was the cries of encouragement coming from her mouth that changed his mind, or the intensity of his own need that drove him forward, it didn't matter. Either way, his thrusts became rough. Urgent. And deep. The desire burning so completely that each cell in her body unfurled, opened, as if spreading wide to accept every ounce of pleasure.

And accept she did, until the heat flared so bright and hot that she came, enveloping her in a blissful blaze that ultimately consumed them both.

The pounding slowly penetrated his consciousness, and, for a moment, Memphis thought the knocking in his head was because he'd had too much to drink. But that had to be wrong, because he could count on one hand the times he'd indulged enough to be hung over. He stirred, momentarily confused. Because if he hadn't had too much to drink, why the aches and pains? Struggling to throw off the lasts remnants of sleep, he took in the carpet beneath him, the blanket over him, and the soft skin of a female body snuggled against him from behind.

Kate.

Suddenly the sore muscles made sense. Memphis sat up, and Kate stirred in her sleep. Careful not to wake her, he disentangled his legs from hers and glanced around the living room. After he'd made love to her in the bedroom, he'd set out to fulfill her wish, starting with the first floor.

They'd made it through three rooms before finally slipping into an exhausted sleep. His lips curled at the memory and he glanced down at Kate, golden hair fanning across the face relaxed in slumber, the scent of lavender lingering in the air. Her lovely naked body was exposed from the waist up, the afghan covering the rest. And judging by the height of the sun at the window, they'd slept late. Memphis was about to pull the blanket away and resume where they'd left off when the pounding came again.

Someone with a persistent hand was at the front door. Hoping the thumping wouldn't wake Kate, Memphis located a second afghan hanging over a chair and wrapped it around his waist, knotting it in the front.

He padded barefoot across the marble floor and pulled open the massive front door, intent on hurrying the interloper away. And then he spied the offending party.

Kate's brother looked as surprised to see Memphis as Memphis was to see him.

"Brian," Memphis said, for lack of anything intelligent to say.

His friend blinked, taking in the rose-colored afghan wrapped around Memphis's waist and then his hair, which was probably standing on end from the number of times Kate had threaded her fingers through it, bringing his head back to her mouth. Or her breast. Or whichever delicious body part he happened to be tending to at the time.

The blank look on Brian's face could have meant anything, and Memphis was beginning to wonder if Kate's brother was going to deck him. And then Brian's expression morphed into a mix of discomfort, doubt and a trace of humor.

"You up for a conversation?" Brian said.

Memphis swiped a hand over his unruly hair. "Coffee," he said, his voice rough, awkward, like the rest of him. "As long as I get coffee first." Though given the situation he hardly needed the extra caffeine jolt.

"Then how about we take this discussion to the kitchen?" Brian said.

Memphis held the door open, and his friend stepped inside. Conscious of Kate sleeping just a room away, Memphis crossed back to quietly pull the living room door closed, praying Brian hadn't caught a glimpse of his sister sleeping on the floor.

He needn't have worried. Because when Memphis turned around he found Brian standing in the middle of the foyer, gazing up the staircase, a look of profound surprise on his face.

The gazillion-thread-count shirt was still draped over the railing. A few steps higher, his pants were piled in a heap. Kate's bra had landed on the massive foyer chandelier that hung from the second-floor ceiling, the scrap of lace dangling alongside the crystal teardrops. But the worst visual of all was the shattered picture that lay facedown on the stairs, fragments of glass littering the steps below.

Awkward instantly upgraded to problematic, and Memphis cleared his throat. "I assume you want coffee, too."

"Yes." Brian shot another glance up the stairs. "Or perhaps a tranquilizer." He raised an eyebrow at Memphis. "Should we be calling the police about a break-in?"

"Not necessary," Memphis said gruffly as he headed down the foyer toward the kitchen, desperate to move past the telltale scene and into safer rooms. "I'll get the coffee started and then go throw on some clothes."

"Or..." Brian leaned down and picked up the silk dress that had been tossed from the second floor. "You could put on this." Memphis narrowed his eyes in response, but Brian didn't have the decency to move along. Kate's brother simply hiked a brow and said, "It couldn't be any more demeaning than your rose-colored afghan with flowers."

Eyeing him warily, Memphis paused, his lips twisting. "I imagine you have more to say than critiquing my current state of attire."

Brian let out a soft scoff, a cross between a confirmation of the understatement and reluctant amusement. He nodded in the direction of the staircase. "Go throw on your clothes while I start the coffee."

Ten minutes later, and a lot more suitably dressed, Memphis entered the massive kitchen done in stainless steel and dark wood, the smell of freshly brewed coffee in the air.

Brian set the carafe on the center island, chic, stainless-steel bar stools lining either side. "I'll get the cream and sugar," he said. "You grab the mugs."

Mugs.

Memphis stared blankly at the wall of mahogany cabinets to his left, assuming that one of them contained the requested items, but having no idea which one.

There was another awkward pause, until Brian spoke from behind. "You know," Brian said. "When I told you to be nice to Kate, this wasn't what I envisioned. And I'm not sure I like the fact you spent the night with my sister but don't have a clue where she keeps her coffee cups."

Memphis turned to look at Brian, who was giving him a mildly teasing look, but packed in there was a whole load of potential for seriousness.

"I didn't realize knowledge of the layout of a kitchen was a prerequisite for involvement with the owner of the house," Memphis said.

Brian's brow furrowed. "It is when the owner of the house is my sister." He nodded to his left. "First cabinet on the end."

Memphis fetched two mugs and returned, taking a seat across from Brian at the center island. "Kate's a grown woman," Memphis said as Brian poured the coffee.

"Hell," Brian said as he set the pot down. "I know that."

Memphis sipped the black coffee, eyeing Brian over the rim of his mug.

"And it's not like we're strangers," Memphis went on. He wasn't ashamed of his actions, and he sure didn't feel the need to explain himself. But Brian was his friend and Kate's brother, and as such the man deserved the courtesy of being allowed to voice his concerns. "We've known each other since I was thirteen."

"Dude," Brian said, his mug suspended in midair, halfway to his mouth. "I was there, remember?" Brian held his gaze for a moment before he said, "That's not what's bothering me."

"So what is?"

Brian heaved out a breath. "Honestly? I think it's fairly obvious. She's at a really vulnerable time in her life, and I'm worried she'll get hurt," he said.

Memphis struggled to suppress his amusement at the irony. Ultimately, if anyone was at risk of coming up on the losing end, it was him. He pushed aside the disturbing thought and sipped his coffee as Brian went on.

"She's already been through the wringer, Memphis. Dalton and Kate had had their ups and downs but things seemed to improve for a while." Brian's brow lowered. "And then the bastard dumped her right after the election."

Memphis choked on his coffee, his coughing fit filling the air as he struggled to rein in his surprise. After finally recovering, he carefully set his mug down. That Kate hadn't come clean about her night with Memphis all those years ago wasn't a shock. That she'd kept the truth about her marriage from her family was.

Why hadn't she told Brian about the extended separation?

"She keeps saying the sudden decision was mutual, but I think she's just protecting Dalton," Brian said. "And if you hurt her I'll feel obligated to throw you off of an eighty-story building, Memphis. Minus the cable," he added pointedly. "With no air bag."

"Brian—"

"You're not around as much as I'd like," Brian went on, and the familiar guilt lurched in Memphis's chest. "But you're still my best friend. And I don't want to have to hurt you."

"Well," Memphis said, shifting uncomfortably in his seat. "I don't want you throwing me off an eighty-story building, either."

"Good," Brian said. "So we're both in agreement."

"One hundred percent." He held Brian's gaze, and the message he saw there left him uneasy. "What exactly did we just agree on?"

Brian's forehead crinkled with vague amusement. "That Kate isn't ready for another relationship yet," Brian said. "And she definitely isn't ready for one with a man who's just blowing through town." He lifted both eyebrows. "And don't even get me started on the problem with my parents."

Inside, Memphis flinched from the hit that knocked him harder than a one-hundred-foot fall.

Brian shook his head softly. "You know how I feel about you, bro."

"Yeah," Memphis said gruffly. He did. Guilt rolled through him, because he didn't deserve the man's dedication. Not after the accident, and not for remaining silent about his sister's marriage. But Kate's story wasn't his to tell. He cleared his throat. "I feel the same way about you."

"My relationship with my parents has improved over the years," Brian said. "But their opinion of you hasn't changed. And Kate's still their favorite child." He leaned forward, his gaze one part apology and one part warning. "She won't be disappointing them."

Memphis gripped his coffee mug, the muscle in his jaw clenching hard. "Well," he said, forcing his fingers to release the handle. He never would have gotten entangled with the woman if she hadn't shown signs of maturing beyond the dutiful daughter who had been too obedient to stand up for herself. "I think I'll let Kate make her own decisions."

He just hoped to hell he hadn't overestimated how much Kate Anderson had changed.

The tantalizing smell of coffee lured Kate from the living room, but the sound of voices coming from the kitchen stopped her in her tracks.

Memphis.

Brian.

Good God. She clutched the blanket tighter around her shoulders, stumped as to what to do next. Her hair was a knotted mass of tangles, and the fabulous night with Memphis had left the faint residue of physical exertion on her skin. She needed a quick shower, some clean clothes and to regain some semblance of dignity before facing the two men in her kitchen.

As she turned to head upstairs she spied the shattered picture frame and her dangling bra. Groaning, she came to a stop, a heated flush of embarrassment washing over her. The blatant evidence of her assertive behavior was bad enough, but the bright light of day made it even worse.

Memphis would never let her live this down.

All she wanted was a cup of coffee and a few minutes alone to recover from the huge step she'd taken last night. Unfortunately, the two men chatting in her kitchen prevented both. As if the messy morning after wasn't awkward enough, she had to endure it with an audience.

Flustered, she cleaned the mess as best she could, frustrated she couldn't retrieve the bra from the chandelier without getting the ladder from the garage. And there was no way she could do that without drawing the attention of the men, so she was forced to leave the undergarment dangling like a banner broadcasting just how hard she'd come undone.

Fifteen minutes later, blessedly clean from her shower and dressed in crop pants and a tailored crepe de chine blouse, Kate entered the kitchen as coolly as she could. As if wild abandoned sex with the world's hottest man happened every day. Maybe she'd get lucky and no one would comment.

"Good to see you, Kate," her brother said dryly. "Sleep well?"

"About time you woke up," Memphis said, his voice a sexy rumble that should have been illegal, even without her brother's presence.

Warmth seeping into her every cell, she smoothed her hand down her blouse and rounded the center island to kiss her brother on the cheek. "Nice of you to drop by, Brian." She cast an awkward glance at Memphis and caught the amused light in his eyes. A kiss-on-the-cheek greeting for him would have been ludicrous at this point. Feeling a need to keep her hands busy, and her back to the two men, she loaded the few items from the sink into the dishwasher. "What's the occasion, big brother?"

He was older than her by two minutes, and normally she loved Brian's company, but today, hurrying him out was the best way to go. She needed to have a discussion with Memphis, and it was the kind her brother really shouldn't be around for. Why was Brian here?

And even more importantly...how long would it take to get him to leave?

"I stopped by because I didn't want you to hear the bad news from someone else," Brian said.

Bad news.

Kate's chest tightened a touch, making her

heart work a little bit harder. Her gaze zeroed in on her brother, and she could sense Memphis's sudden attention as well as he sat up higher in his seat.

Struggling to remain calm, she picked up the spoon Brian had used to stir his coffee and placed it in the dishwasher. "Which bad news would that be?" Kate said, holding her breath.

Brian pursed his lips. "It might be easier to show you."

As if preparing for the event, Kate's heart shifted lower in her chest as Brian crossed to her laptop on the kitchen counter. He carried it over, setting it on the marble-topped center island.

Brian tapped a few keys on the keyboard, and the high-school-reunion website came into view. Kate's heart sank a little lower.

She had a feeling she knew what would come next. "If this is about—"

The high-school picture of her and Dalton popped onto the page, cutting off her words. Kate stared at the image of her in the ridiculous tiara next to Dalton in his matching crown. His and hers coronets. The smiles on their faces were brilliant, despite the silly headgear, and for a moment the feelings rolled through her. It had, without a doubt, been the happiest moment of her life. Even on the day of her wedding she'd had a vague feeling of unease. But she'd passed that off as prenuptial jitters.

And how sad was it that her life had peaked in high school?

She sucked in a breath. *Dear God, let it not be a continual downhill slide from here.* "I already heard about the picture, Brian."

"But have you seen the comments?" her brother said.

Comments.

Kate pressed her thumb and forefinger to her forehead, hoping the hints at a pounding headache weren't a promise of things to come. The stupid website, a maneuver she'd considered a necessary addition to the reunion preparations, was beginning to be the bane of her existence. The committee had considered it a fabulous move. Mostly the site was fabulous at being a meeting place for those community members who'd wished to carry on a discussion about her and Dalton, usually precipitated by the tabloid headlines.

"What's the discussion today?" she said apprehensively.

"How you and Dalton are going to manage the reunion festivities."

"What do you mean?" she said. Her heart already around the level of her belly, there didn't seem much farther for it to go.

She was wrong.

"A reporter asked Dalton about the reunion," Brian went on. "Apparently your ex and his fiancée will be attending."

She stared at her brother, who really should have looked more alarmed while delivering the unwelcome news. "But Dalton and I discussed this. He said he didn't want to go."

Brian scowled. "It seems he has changed his mind. He probably figures acting as if everything was normal is a way to get beyond the bad press."

Her heart reached her toes and wedged tight. There just wasn't any room to move lower.

Memphis cleared his throat. "Could make the reunion a little awkward."

Kate sent him a wide-eyed look that most likely telegraphed the panic she was feeling. "You think?"

After an assessing gaze, Memphis crossed the kitchen and retrieved a mug from the cabinet, filled it with coffee and set it in front of her. "Cream or sugar?" he asked, as if that was the biggest dilemma she had to deal with today.

"A shot of whiskey, please. No, wait," she said, wrapping her cold fingers around the warm ceramic mug. "Make that two shots."

Memphis's mouth twitched. "I'd suggest you stick with cream."

He poured a dollop of the oh-so-insufficient addition into her coffee, and Kate inhaled a fortifying whiff of the brew, letting the wonderful smell wash through her before taking a sip.

"Okay," she said, setting her mug down and hoping she was ready. "What kind of comments are on the web page, anyway?"

Brian raised a brow. "You really want to know?

If she was going to listen to the murmurs behind her back at the cocktail party next week, she wanted to be able to take them in context. "Fire away."

"They call her the replacement wife."

"So what does that make me?" Kate said.

"Obsolete?" Memphis suggested helpfully, and she shot him a look.

"I'm only twenty-eight years old," she said. "Surely that's too young to be considered obsolete."

"That's not all," Brian went on.

"What else could there possibly be to discuss?" Kate said.

"Plenty, apparently," Brian said. "But the biggest discussion by far is how you, Dalton and his new lady are going to navigate the two social functions at the reunion."

Kate closed her eyes and inhaled deeply. Lovely. Now the town was arguing about how she should schedule her social calendar. "Any decent suggestions that I can use?" she said, her lips quirking wryly.

Brian scrolled through the screen while Memphis stood behind him, arm braced against the counter, reading over her brother's shoulder. Kate couldn't look.

"The comments fall into two camps, the serious and the absurd." Brian scanned the text for a moment. "One lady suggested you two should divide up the night."

"Sounds civilized," Memphis said, shooting her a mocking smile. "Right up Kate's alley."

Kate's lips flattened, and her brother ignored

Memphis and went on. "Another suggested you two should divide the reception hall in half and each stick to your own side."

Memphis shot her a serious look he clearly didn't feel. "I'd suggest you take the half with the restroom."

"Funny," Kate said, hoping her look communicated just how much she wasn't amused.

Brian scrunched up his face. "Which begs the question, what is the minimum safe distance between you and your bastard of an ex, anyway?"

Memphis swiped a hand down his face, clearly fighting to hold back a smile. "Kate and I were just having a similar discussion last night at the dinner party." His eyes were hot as they met hers over her brother's head, sending goose bumps prickling down her back. "Except our discussion was about where my hand—"

"Enough," Kate said as she closed the laptop computer with a resounding *thunk,* ignoring the traitorous thrum of desire that begged for more of Memphis.

After last night her body was beyond willing, but her mind was still convinced it was a mistake to want more, and her heart couldn't stand the infighting. And by the look on Memphis's face, the one that said he was ready to pick up where they'd left off—which probably meant the kitchen—once Brian was gone, her mission was going to get more difficult.

Amused, Memphis held her gaze.

Without looking at her brother, Kate said, "Brian, I need to have a discussion with Memphis." She turned her gaze to Brian. "Alone, please."

CHAPTER SEVEN

SENSING he wasn't going to like what came next, Memphis stared at Kate. She had a we-need-to-have-a-conversation look that was the total antithesis of his which-room-next? thoughts.

"Brian, please," Kate said.

Her brother pushed back in his chair and stood. "Okay," he said, drawing out the vowels in the word as if buying time to think.

Kate didn't allow him the luxury. She took his arm, steering him toward the hallway. "Thanks for the warning about the comments. I'll walk you to the door." As they all entered the foyer, heading for the front entrance, Kate said, "Give me a call later, okay?"

Brian looked up at the bra on the chandelier. "You need help getting that down?"

Kate kept her eyes straight ahead, escorting her brother toward the front door. "Memphis will take care of it."

"I don't remember agreeing to that," Memphis said, and Kate shot him a look behind her brother's back, but Memphis simply crinkled his forehead in amusement.

Brian turned at the front entrance. "I can help—"

"I love you, Brian." Kate opened the door and gently pushed him out onto the stoop. "Now leave," she said as she closed the door in his face.

Memphis lifted a brow, biting back the grin. "That was rude."

"He's my brother. Occasional rudeness is to be expected and is always forgiven."

"No need to apologize to me, either," he said. He let his voice drop an octave. "I like it when you get pushy."

Her lips pressed in a flat line and she crossed her arms, as if bracing for the conversation. Without bothering to look in the direction of her bra, she said, "Will you help me get that down?"

Clearly she didn't like the lingering evidence of their previous escapades.

He glanced at the scrap of white lace dangling like a living, though certainly not breathing, reminder of just how out of control they'd been last night. How out of control *she* had been.

Not that anyone would know to look at Kate now. Her casual pants and delicate blouse were simple, though no doubt designer. And, combined with her sleek blond hair, her presentation was so chic and cool it screamed "do not bother unwrapping, ice princess inside" to anyone who braved a closer look.

As far as he figured it, he knew her better than most.

But given how much she'd kept from her family, perhaps it was time to delve deeper. His curiosity had grown too acute to ignore anymore. Was her reserve simply a byproduct of her upbringing? Or was there something more to her habit of coolly encasing her emotions in ice?

Either way, it was past time Memphis discovered the full truth.

Because he'd finally experienced her raw sexuality and had been pleased as hell. The wildly abandoned Kate had surpassed even his best teenage fantasies. He would never be satisfied with a single night, but he also wanted more than just hot sex with a woman he didn't understand.

And that meant prying the lid off her intriguingly cool facade.

"I think the bra looks nice there," he said, stepping closer. He sensed, rather than saw her straighten her back. Gathering those defenses. "It reminds me that there is a real Kate living beneath that careful exterior of yours."

She blinked hard. Twice. And then three more times. He wondered if every time she opened her eyes she was disappointed he was still there.

Finally, she said, "The ladder is in the garage."

"At least give the interesting decoration a day to grow on you."

Ignoring his statement, she headed back up the foyer. "I have several different kinds, including a folding ladder and a stepladder," she said. "I'm sure you can find one that will work."

"It *is* an obnoxiously sized chandelier," he said. "So the proportions are off with just the bra. But if you tossed the matching panties up there, it would balance out the look."

"Just be careful to set your equipment up properly," she went on smoothly, a dignified sarcasm to her tone. "We wouldn't want you to fall and break your neck."

"Maybe you also need a couple of garters to go along with them, as well." Amused, he followed her through what appeared to be a utility room and into the garage. "Though that might be a bit much."

"Because climbing up an ordinary piece of equipment should not lead to Hollywood's premier high-fall stuntman crashing to his death," she went on.

"I'd be happy to pitch in for the cost of the garters."

"How embarrassing would that obituary be?" she returned smoothly, though her gaze cut through him like a jagged icicle.

Memphis bit back the smile and then took a moment to look around the garage, her single luxurious sedan lost in the five-car space. Everything was stored neatly and in its proper place. Hell, the floor looked so clean you could probably eat off it without experiencing the tiniest bit of gritty crunch between your teeth. Order and cleanliness inside a home was reasonable, he supposed. But in a garage, it was unnatural.

Chin just high enough to show she meant business, Kate pointed at the line of ladders hung neatly on the far wall. "Take your pick."

Memphis heaved out an exaggerated breath of defeat. "I'm crushed you're ignoring my decorating tips." He lifted an aluminum ladder off its hooks, resting it on his shoulder. Kate headed back through the utility room, and Memphis followed, his tone amused again. "Why do I get the feeling I'm being treated like a schoolkid being told to clean up the mess I made?"

"Because you are," she said as she fell into step beside him. "You're the one who tossed the bra aside."

He shot her a look between the rungs of the ladder. "But you were the one who shattered a picture frame."

"And I've cleaned up my mess," she said, stopping beneath the chandelier and pointing up at the bra. "It's only fair you clean up yours."

He set up the folding ladder beneath the chandelier. "I'm going to change your nickname from Angel Face to Kill Joy," he muttered, climbing the steps.

He reached for the bra, trying to lift it from the sea of pointed crystal prisms dangling just above his head. After a minute or two of adjusting the angle of his attempt, the lacy undergarment still refused to budge.

"It's stuck," he said. "Apparently the bra wants to stay."

"Memphis," Kate said, the long-suffering tone in her voice slipping a bit. "Do not mess with me. The caterer is coming this afternoon to finalize some details for the reunion." She cast a worried glance at the bra. "I cannot have my chandelier playing dress-up when she arrives."

He heard the brittle tone of her voice and finally dislodged the bra, turning to park his hip on the top rung of the ladder and look down at the woman below. Something bigger than an inappropriately attired fixture was eating at Kate. "Are you bothered by how hard you came on to me last night?"

She stared up at him, her voice soft. "No."

Satisfied, he pushed a little further. "Are you going to make love to me again?"

This time her response was firm. "No."

"Why not?"

Her voice was irritatingly reasonable, as if she'd memorized her answer in advance. "I'm only twenty-eight years old, Memphis," she said. "And I've already made enough mistakes in my life to fill a novel. I know Dalton made some serious mistakes, too." She laid a hand on her chest, honesty radiating from her eyes. "But ultimately it's my decisions, *my* actions, that I have to live with. And I'm going to do everything in my power to keep future regrets to a minimum."

"That sounds like a hell of a boring way to live."

"Not all of us are built for the thrill like you."

"You can't spend the rest of your life making up for past mistakes," he said. "Regrets are useless."

She let out a faint scoff. "Those who say never to waste your life on regrets have either never made any large enough to count or are just plain selfish."

Memphis studied her for a moment before descending the ladder, bra in hand. He came to a halt at the bottom, tipping his head. "There is nothing wrong with occasional selfishness, Kate."

She paused before responding with another answer that felt rehearsed. "You—" she pointed at him "—and me," she went on, placing a hand on her chest. "We're messy. Complicated." She smoothed a hand across her cheek. "And right now I *really* need simple."

In view of everything she'd been through, the statement was hard to argue with. Memphis met her gaze, taking in the blue eyes and the sleek loop of hair at her neck. Kate liked her life pretty, neat and organized. She didn't like messes, whether the literal ones on a staircase or the emotional ones being dragged through the media.

And *complicated* defined their relationship.

"Is that why you lied to your family about the end of your marriage?" he said as he stepped closer to Kate. "Because it was simpler?"

From the shocked look on her face it was clear she hadn't prepared for this particular question. The awkwardness rolled off Kate as her expression morphed through a range of emotions before she finally responded.

"I was trying to spare them," she said.

"Spare them?" His brow bunched. "These are your parents we're talking about. And *Brian*."

"I couldn't expect my family to pretend everything was okay between me and Dalton during the election campaign. It was a burden I'd accepted for myself, not for them."

Bra in hand, he crossed his arms, refusing to let her off easy. Digging for the truth was too important. And the look on his face must have telegraphed his skepticism.

With a sigh, Kate rubbed her temple, shifting her gaze to stare down the hallway. The seconds ticked by before she went on. "Succeeding in high school was easy for me," she said in a low voice. "Succeeding in college was easy, too. My marriage was the first real failure in my life, Memphis. And I felt so…" She briefly pressed her lids closed before dropping her arm and turning to look at him again, her eyes now bubbling with a bleak emotion that knifed him in the chest. "Ashamed."

Working hard to keep his heart from bleeding too much, he reached out to cup her face. "There is no shame in failure, Kate," he said as he smoothed his thumb across her cheek, holding her gaze and trying to impress upon her the importance of his words. "You've got to cut yourself some slack."

Time stretched as he enjoyed her silky skin.

And slowly, what had started as a comfort shifted to something more, and his body began to hum with remembered desire, delighting in the emerging signs her body was, too. The slightly widened eyes appeared first. And then came the rapid rate of the rise and fall of her very feminine chest. Finally a touch of color crept up her cheeks.

When she shifted her head slightly, breaking their contact, he dropped his hand. "Angel Face," he said dryly. "I am not the enemy."

"I never said you were."

With a wry hike of his brow, he said, "And I can't be just your friend, either."

"So what title would you suggest?"

After a pause, Memphis held up her bra, dangling her lingerie from his finger. "How about frenemies with benefits?"

The furrow lining her brow grew deeper as she swept the garment from his hand. "No more benefits," she said, her lips twisting with a frustration that was clearly self-directed. "You make me do things out of character."

"Do I?" he said, reaching up to trace her collarbone. He heard her breath catch and, in that moment he relived every sound that had come from her mouth the night before. "I bet I can convince you otherwise."

"Sorry, Memphis," she said. "I'm not going to give you the chance."

One week later Kate gripped her clutch purse and smoothed a hand down her cocktail dress, hungry, but too nervous for appetizers. As far as evenings went, Kate had had better. But the recent arrival of Tabitha Reed at her side meant the party was about to get worse.

"I like your choice of a date, Kate." Tabitha's green cat eyes were fixed on Memphis as he mingled with the guests on the far side of the chic living room of Cheryl Jackson's home. As hosts, the Jacksons were gracious, and one of the few couples present Kate considered real friends. Tabitha Reed certainly wasn't. "He is absolutely delish," Tabitha went on.

"I suppose," Kate murmured noncommittally, studying Memphis as he spoke with Tabitha's husband. As much as Kate hated to, she agreed with the woman's assessment.

No man, no matter the clothes, compared. The simple dress shirt and pants perfectly displayed his athletic physique. Toss in the lopsided smile and a girl was a goner—because that smile frequently transformed into a grin of sensual memory that could melt butter faster than a fiery griddle. But it was the eyes that did Kate in. She no longer thought of them as caramel-colored, because that description was entirely too sweet. No, the rational-thought-slaying effect of his gaze could only be described as closer to a shade of intoxicating whiskey.

Tabitha said, "Is he as good in bed as he looks?"

Better.

Kate pushed aside the surge of memories

and ignored the trace of guilt the tiny white lie brought. "I couldn't say."

Tabitha's head whipped to face Kate, her stylish, chin-length black hair swinging around her elfin face. "You don't know?"

Technically it was the truth, because she and Memphis had never actually had sex in a bed. Years ago the living-room sofa was as far as they'd made it before falling into an exhausted sleep. After her bedroom carpet last week, Memphis had set out to fulfill her wish of making love to her in every room, starting with the bottom story of her home. And there were no beds on the first floor.

The disbelieving look on Tabitha's face was comical.

"No, I don't know," Kate said as she struggled to keep from laughing. "We're just friends," she added, hoping her coolly spoken words would bring an end to the woman's need to share her opinion.

But Tabitha Reed had opinion to spare. "You can tell me the truth."

Kate's smile grew tighter. "I am."

The woman raised an overplucked brow. "Listen, hon, we need to talk. After everything you went through with Dalton, I'm worried about you."

"I appreciate your concern," Kate said, hoping the droll tone wasn't noticeable. "But I'm fine." Tabitha's eyebrow remained sky-high, no hint of returning to ground level any time soon. *"Really,"* Kate added for emphasis.

"Girl, you have got to get back out there," Tabitha went on as if Kate hadn't spoken, her eyes settling back on Memphis. "And the delectable Mr. James is the perfect transition man."

The label caught Kate by surprise. The term seemed too tame to apply to Memphis. "Transition man?"

Tabitha let out a long-suffering sigh, as if she had much to teach her, and Kate was surprised the woman didn't refer to her as her young apprentice. "Kate, you need to get with the divorce program. A transition man is a good-time guy who clearly isn't marriage material. One who has no interest in a long-term relationship." A smile crawled up Tabitha's face as she stared at Memphis. "A transition man offers the freedom of not having to worry about whether he's the right man, or good for you, or whether he has enough money or not." She flicked a diamond-studded hand. "Or all those other serious dating dilemmas."

"I never considered money—"

"They offer fun times, lots of laughs," Tabitha said, ignoring Kate's response. "And great sex." She glanced back at Kate. "And you look like you could use all three."

Kate blinked, stumped as to how to respond to the woman's crass critique. Of course, it didn't help that Kate was still struggling to recover from having really great sex with Memphis.

She swallowed hard, gathering her composure. "I appreciate the concern, Tabitha," Kate said smoothly. "But I've known Memphis since I was a teen." And because she'd done everything in her power to label him as a friend at the first dinner party, Memphis was now considered fair game by any and every single female in the room, and a few of the married ones, as well. "He is simply my brother's best friend."

As if sensing her lie from across the room, Memphis turned his head, and their gazes locked. The look was so hot that the fifteen feet separating them felt like fifteen inches, frying every one of her nerve endings. The resulting dizzying sensation made her clutch her purse harder, heat curling the edges of her every cell.

"I think you forgot to tell the man he's only a friend. And remember, Kate," murmured Tabitha, leaning close as if departing great wisdom. "Carpe diem."

And then Tabitha headed off, leaving Kate trapped in Memphis's gaze.

Given the hand-placement debate during their last public performance, and knowing she'd never be able to function if he was touching her again, as soon as they'd arrived at the party tonight she'd shooed him away. She'd made the perfunctory rounds of the guests with the sole intent of meeting her social obligations as quickly as possible. Hanging out with Memphis was dangerous. His smoldering looks alone were enough to muck with her cool demeanor.

Like the forceful pull of a swirling maelstrom, Memphis's gaze continued to hold hers, and Tabitha's words came back to taunt Kate. The concept of relaxing and indulging in a sexy man's company was incredibly tempting. The months of strain, of pretending that she and Dalton were a united front—especially in front of her family—had worn her down the way a swift current erodes a riverbank.

If Memphis had been anyone else she might have made the decision to go with the flow after the sizzling night they'd spent in her house. But even though the man defined temptation, his gaze more tantalizingly sinful than the seven deadly sins combined, he was still Memphis James.

And there was no escaping their past. Or her mistake.

Memphis continued to unbalance her from across the room, his eyes traveling over her form with appreciation, revving up her heart, and Kate's palms grew damp against her clutch purse. Maintaining a collected air was critical, but with every passing second Memphis seduced her from afar—until she felt the need to escape lest she pool into a molten puddle on the floor.

In search of a moment of peace, Kate turned on her heel and headed out of the living room and down the hall, away from the chatter of the party and into the seclusion of Ted Jackson's den. On the far side of the room a door was cracked open, a sink visible beyond. Blowing out a breath of relief, Kate passed through the den, the walls lined with pictures of a large fishing boat. She entered the bathroom, turned on the tap, and stuck her hands under the water, nearly groaning out loud in approval.

The quiet was calming. The cool water was soothing. And she didn't feel so hot and bothered anymore, so Kate turned off the tap. Just as she was beginning to enjoy the peace and quiet, she heard female voices.

"Poor thing," a woman said as she entered the den on the other side of the door. "She must feel so abandoned."

"I know," Tabitha's voice replied, and several female voices murmured in agreement. "It's not like she had a life outside her marriage."

Kate's heart freeze-dried in her chest and crumbled, a powerful sense of dread overtaking her. It was bad enough being talked about behind her back, but she had no desire to hear exactly what people were saying—especially when the only thing between them was a partially open door that blocked her from view.

"It's hard to feel sorry for her, though," the first voice went on.

"Personally, I don't think she appreciated what she had with Dalton." Tabitha Reed's tone was without sympathy. "Everything always went her way, and she has no idea how to cope now that it's not."

Kate was half tempted to walk in on them, just to watch their faces burn with embarrassment. But confrontation wasn't the goal. The goal of the evening was to survive with as few ripples as possible. Confronting the gossip girls would be horribly awkward.

Debating her next move, she closed her eyes. Waiting for them to move on and then finishing her social obligations before making a dignified exit seemed the wisest course of action. Unless one of them decided to use the facilities…

The only thing more awkward than confronting them directly would be getting caught cowering in the bathroom.

Unfortunately, it was past time to make an appearance, and the women seemed in no hurry to leave as they continued to chat about her inability to cope.

"Kate needs to get a life outside of being Mrs. Dalton Worthington," Tabitha said, her tone showing no signs of tiring of the subject. "And she's a fool for not taking advantage of the gorgeous Mr. James."

Memphis.

Heart pounding, a plan swirling into place, Kate reached in her purse for her cellphone, punching the keyboard and texting: *I need your help.*

Memphis was dealing with two fawning females and an enthusiastic action-film fan determined to describe Memphis's every stunt when his cellular beeped. Grateful for the interruption, Memphis pulled out his phone and read the message—and a knot of irritation coiled in his chest.

He was at the pretentious function because he'd agreed to help Kate out. And yet, despite a night of spectacular passion—after which she'd told him it couldn't be repeated—she'd dragged him here and then dropped him like a hot and heavy stone. Practically pretended he didn't exist. Now she needed his assistance again and suddenly she was acknowledging his presence.

Memphis stared at the text message asking for his assistance and contemplated how to respond. Several seconds later, he typed: *Happy to help. Which bedroom shall I meet you in?*

Memphis held back the smile as he imagined Kate biting her lip in irritation. It served her right, especially after avoiding him tonight as though he was the proverbial plague. Several seconds ticked by, and he knew she was wrestling with her annoyance, trying to find a politically correct response.

She texted: *That's not the kind of help I need.*

Memphis finally let a smile slip up his face as he sent another response. *It was the other night.*

During the pause that followed, Memphis pictured steam coming from Kate's ears as she fought to maintain that ever-present cool expression. Feeling the need to goad her further, to at least get an honest response from her, Memphis typed another message. *I noticed that the Jacksons' chandelier looks a little plain. Are you interested in donating your bra to a worthy cause?*

Several heartbeats passed before she responded: *Although that sounds like fun...* Despite missing out on her tone, Memphis knew the words were dripping with sarcasm. *The sad truth is, Mr. James, that I'm not wearing one.*

The text was punctuated with a slyly smirking emoticon, and Memphis knew she was taunting him back. So he texted: *I think I should verify the lack of proper underwear for myself.*

Her reply was quick. *Instead, maybe you should pretend you have manners and help your friend in need?*

Do you promise to tear my shirt from my chest if I do?

Another lengthy pause followed, and Memphis hoped he would experience Kate's first cussword via text message.

Her response was a huge disappointment. *Are you going to help me or not?*

So much for profanity. He typed: *What's the problem?*

Tabitha and her friends have me trapped in the bathroom in the den.

How the heck could they have her trapped? Memphis texted a simple question mark.

They're talking about me. There was a pause before she texted more. *And you.*

Memphis's brow scrunched in amusement. *Are they saying nice things about me?*

The text *Memphis!* was followed by several punctuation marks mimicking a barrage of cusswords, and he let out a chuckle. It was rather sadistic of him, being pleased he'd frustrated her as much as she was frustrating the hell out of him.

But there was something about Kate's ability to walk away from him, about her parents' long-held belief in his inferiority, and this town's surprise at his professional success that cranked up his usual don't-give-a-damn attitude to in-your-face supreme.

Resurrecting bad memories.

Because, while growing up, it hadn't mattered he wasn't a drug dealer or a gang member, he was from a seedy neighborhood so people assumed he was trouble. It hadn't mattered that he'd earned a grade point average to be proud of, he'd attended the wrong high school so the grades didn't count. And when a single mistake had almost gotten his best friend killed, few in town were shocked, because what more could one expect from someone like Memphis James?

Staring down at his phone, he pushed the old resentment away, focusing on his current dilemma. Kate was neither fragile nor a coward. The gracious way she'd handled the press so far was admirable. But for some reason she had a thing about conflict, going out of her way to avoid confrontation. And that included the habit of emotionally retreating from him. He supposed he should rescue the fair maiden yet again. But that didn't mean he couldn't use her predicament to find out what made her tick…and enjoy himself in the process.

A smile curled on his lips as he texted: *I'm on my way.*

CHAPTER EIGHT

"I HEARD Dalton's fiancée has worked for him for the past two years," Tabitha Reed said, her interpretation of *that* piece of news clear in her tone of voice.

Blowing out a breath, Kate quietly closed the lid to the toilet and took a seat, crossing her legs. What was taking Memphis so long? She was dying of thirst, her stomach was growling with hunger and if she had to spend another nanosecond in the enclosed walls of this bathroom she was going to go stark raving mad.

Unfortunately, Tabitha droned on. "As soon as Dalton established himself politically, he dumped Kate for a—"

"Good evening, ladies."

At the sound of Memphis's voice, Kate breathed a sigh of relief. Thank God the nightmare was over.

"Sorry. I didn't mean to interrupt," he went on. There was a faint scrunching sound, like someone taking a seat on one of the leather chairs in the den. "Dumped Kate for a what, Tabitha?"

Kate recognized the challenge in his voice—God knows she'd encountered it a million times before—and dismay shot through her like a torpedo. He couldn't. He *wouldn't*. She squeezed her eyes shut, hoping she'd heard him incorrectly.

"I'd love to hear the rest," he went on easily.

Of course he would, because Memphis James did whatever he wanted.

And right now he didn't care how long she'd been trapped. He wanted to provoke the women who had spent the past fifteen minutes analyzing every detail of Kate's marriage, minus the bothersome nuisance of actual facts, of course. Kate fisted the hand in her lap. So much for escaping her tiny prison. Next time she hid out while people talked about her, she wouldn't text the maddening hell-raiser for help.

Kate could feel the awkward silence from here.

"He dumped Kate for a trophy wife," Tabitha finally said, her voice cool.

A trophy wife? Kate's lids stretched wide. Is that how the public viewed the soon-to-be new Mrs. Worthington? And how was it possible at twenty-eight years of age to be replaced by a trophy wife? It had to be a new world record.

"And you're basing this assumption on…?" Memphis said.

There was another pause before Tabitha spoke. "Everyone knows the only reason Dalton married Kate was for her political family name."

Kate raised her brow. Amazing what one heard about one's marriage from other people.

"That's interesting," Memphis went on smoothly, though his tone contained a thread of steel. "Dalton told you this himself?"

"No, of course not," Tabitha replied. For the first time she sounded flustered.

"But you're basing this knowledge on actual facts, I hope," Memphis said dryly.

There was an extended pause, and despite the tension gripping her back, Kate couldn't prevent the smile from creeping up her face.

"Well," Tabitha said, her voice defensive. "I find it awfully convenient he dumped Kate for a younger woman right after the election."

"So, should I assume the worst about your husband, as well?"

"Excuse me?" Tabitha said, sounding shocked.

Memphis didn't miss a beat. "No, I don't think I will," he went on smoothly, not sounding the slightest bit contrite. "But seeing how your husband left the living room at the exact same time as the pretty woman who was enjoying his latest fishing tale, I suppose I could assume he's off for some monkey business of his own."

The noise that followed was like a tiny strangled sound coming from a malfunctioning throat, and the next thing Kate heard was the sound of movement out of the den. No doubt Tabitha's groupies followed her out the door.

When Memphis entered the bathroom, Kate shot to her feet and lightly jabbed his arm. "Memphis," she hissed, relief and frustration so tightly entwined she wasn't sure what to say next.

Memphis closed the door behind him. "Is that the thanks I get for chasing your captors away?"

She sagged against the bathroom counter. "I *am* grateful," she said. "But next time will you please not settle into a comfortable seat and proceed to prolong my torture by antagonizing my jailors?" She narrowed her eyes curiously at Memphis. "Did Tabitha's husband really sneak off with one of the guests?"

"Not exactly," he said as he propped a shoulder against the wall looking relaxed. Watchful. And terribly amused. Unfortunately, there was also something in his eyes that screamed trouble. Instantly the tiny room shrank to the size of a teacup, his muscular frame filling every available space. "I think the woman in question left to find her date while Tabitha's husband left with Ted Jackson to admire his boat in the garage." He lifted a brow. "So unless he goes both ways, the malicious gossiper is safe from a pending infidelity scandal."

Kate smoothed a hand down her dress, gathering her scrambled nerves. She really needed to acknowledge his help, finish her socializing responsibilities and get out of this house. "Thank you, Memphis," she said. "You saved me from a potentially embarrassing moment."

"Actually," he said, his voice dropping to a throaty rumble. "I didn't come to save you."

She steeled herself against the sensual tone, refusing to ask why he'd come. She was positive nothing helpful would spring from his mouth.

He went on as if she'd asked anyway. "I came because I wanted to confirm your previous statement." He took a half step closer, which was enough to rob her of her breath and leave her drowning in those whiskey-colored eyes.

"Which statement?" she said.

"The one where you said you weren't wearing a bra," he continued, and heat flooded her belly before seeping lower—a sensation not unlike downing a shot of alcohol.

Note to self: never tease Memphis James, even if he is several rooms away and you feel safe.

But she'd had enough cowering for one day. Kate lifted her chin and said, "My dress has a built-in bra. And you are not feeling me up in Cheryl Jackson's bathroom."

Ignoring the warning tone in her voice, he said, "I'm not?"

"No," she said firmly. "And furthermore..." Her words trailed off as Memphis reached out and traced the off-the-shoulder, crisscrossing lace neckline of her dress, and desire shot to her every corner. "I want to finish my duties here and leave."

"But the party has just gotten interesting."

"If you call being trapped in a bathroom interesting."

"It depends on who you're trapped with," he said, his eyes growing darker. "And what you're doing."

Kate placed a hand on his chest with the intent

of holding him back, ignoring the hard muscle beneath the shirt. "Memphis, I really want to leave."

"We're not leaving until you acknowledge my presence."

"What are you talking about?"

"You've been ignoring me all evening."

She stared up at him, her heart thumping its approval at Memphis's matching rhythm beneath her hand. "I haven't been—"

"You haven't spoken two words to me since we walked through that front door," he said, his tone low. Kate wasn't sure if she heard irritation or desire in his voice, but she got the impression it might be both. "I'm not a convenience to pull out when you need help or…" His tone dropped another octave. "Or when you're feeling alone and needy."

God help her, she was feeling needy all right.

"I didn't mean to ignore you," she said. And it was the truth. "I was just trying to make tonight easier."

The doubtful look on his face was small, but significant. "Kate, you think too much. And easier on whom? Me?" He stepped closer, and his scent filled her senses, his handsome face filled her view. "Or you?"

Heart pounding, she dropped her gaze in defense. Unfortunately that meant she was staring at the chest that had fascinated her since her teen years. The lean, lanky torso of adolescence had filled out into the wall of well-cut muscle of adulthood. Her body insisted he was right, she was thinking too much. But her mind kept reminding her of her goals to keep things simple and easy. To get through the reunion with as much dignity as possible, and, above all else, to get her messed-up life back on track. And for goodness' sake, that included no repetition of past mistakes.

Memphis was never easy. Nothing about their relationship was simple. And he was her biggest mistake. A gorgeous, sexy reminder of just how far off track her life could get if she followed anything other than her brain.

"I was trying to make it easier on me, of course," she said, forcing herself to meet his gaze and hoping the honesty would help her cause. But she was a little embarrassed by the amount of distress and desperation that seeped into her voice. "I just can't *think* straight when you're around, Memphis."

His eyes locked with hers, the moment stretching forever as she waited for his response, and then a dark look crossed his face.

"Christ, Kate," Memphis muttered, the frustration clear in his voice. "You're not the only one."

He covered her mouth with his, and a tiny breath caught in her throat—a small sound that spoke volumes. He didn't demand. The kiss wasn't angry, and neither was it a punishment for ignoring him. If it had been any of these she would have pushed him away.

Instead, it was the touch of a man who wanted a woman and wasn't able to deny himself. Which made it impossible to resist, and Kate sighed, parting her lips in welcome.

His response was immediate, cupping her face with his hands and tipping her head to capture more of her mouth. His lips and tongue slanted across hers as if he couldn't get enough of the contact, and Kate nearly groaned out loud from the simple pleasure.

During the first two years of her marriage the sex had been good, though sparse, and the pleasure had steadily waned thereafter as Dalton's time constraints grew. Until Kate had withered from the neglect. After she'd confessed to Dalton about her night with Memphis it had been a long time before her husband had touched her again. And from then on his sparse attentions had felt more like duty than desire. But with Memphis, she always felt wanted.

And there was nothing more powerful than feeling too irresistible to ignore.

She met him kiss for kiss and fumbled with the buttons of his shirt. When she finally parted the expensive covering, she ran her hands over his chest, allowing herself the freedom to explore every dip, every bulge—the ridges of hard muscle and sinew. She found and traced the scar low on his flat abdomen, and a small groan escaped Memphis's throat, no doubt in remembered pleasure.

She pulled her mouth away.

"Kate," Memphis said, his voice hoarse, full of frustration.

Until she placed her mouth on the puckered scar on his collarbone.

"Kate." This time his gruff voice was low, full of approval.

Her lips traced the well-healed scar and then moved lower, relishing the warm, salty skin. Making love to Memphis was always exhilarating, one of the few times his I-don't-give-a-damn attitude and love for danger were an asset. Her whole life had been spent toeing the line, and this wild, risk-loving man pushed her to the boundaries and beyond. It was a powerfully addicting feeling.

When her mouth brushed across a flat nipple, Memphis sucked in a breath, cupping her head to hold her close. She smoothed her palms across his taut abdomen and slowly knelt to the floor, her lips moving to the old burn on his left flank. Kate's fingers unfastened his belt. Once she had him unbuckled, she moved on to the front of his pants, her tongue tracing the scar just beneath his navel.

The hiss from Memphis melted her to the core.

Longing for closer contact, Kate pulled out his erection and began to lavish as much attention on the hard length as she had on each individual scar, her lips and tongue paying homage to every inch. Memphis moaned and clasped her head tighter in encouragement, and need wound tight between her legs, leaving her hot. Damp. The harsh breaths coming from Memphis's throat spurred her on, made her feel reckless, and *alive*—her only thought to bring him to completion.

But Memphis, apparently, had other plans.

"Not yet, Angel Face," he murmured, and he hauled her to her feet, his mouth landing on hers. The kiss that followed was raw, rough, but unhurried as he pushed her off-the-shoulder sleeves down her arms, leaving her breasts exposed. He took a moment to run his palms over the curves, calloused skin moving across her tips. Desire curled tight in her belly, desire that only grew stronger as he slid the hem of her dress up to her hips and cupped her buttocks, lifting her onto the bathroom counter.

When he bent her back over his arm, sanity briefly tried to take over Kate, and she murmured. "This is crazy—"

His mouth landed on a nipple, and fire and melted steel coursed through her veins, her tip swelling in response. Kate sucked in a breath, dropping her head back.

Just a few more minutes. Just a few, and then I'll—

Memphis scraped his teeth across a tip, and pleasure engulfed her. She threaded her fingers through his hair, encouraging him as he divided his time between her breasts, lavishing attention on one before moving back to the other. Until she was so hot and so bothered and so ready for him she didn't protest when Memphis gripped her buttock, her thigh draped over his forearm, and swept aside the crotch of her undies. Heated gaze on hers, he thrust inside.

"Memphis," she whispered, closing her eyes in delight.

He arched between her legs again, his voice gruff. "I'm not stopping."

"I don't want you to," she whispered. "But we should go—"

"We're not going anywhere," he said, and rocked his hips again.

Pleasure welled higher, and a soft groan escaped her lips. "I'm not sure I can be quiet."

"Then let me help you with that." And he lowered his head for a kiss.

Mouth fused with hers, one hand on her buttocks, Memphis made love to her with a determination that was electrifying. And, despite their surroundings, he was in no hurry. Memphis James took what Memphis James wanted.

And right now, he wanted Kate.

The pace was slow, unhurried, yet with a dark desire and a hint of desperation stamped in his every movement. Until Kate dug her nails into his shoulders, egging him on. Begging for more. Urging him to go faster. The only noise in the room was the tiny strangled sound of satisfaction that escaped her throat. And when Memphis finally succumbed to her near-silent pleas, his thrusts now hurried and aching with need, the building pressure of pleasure burst upward and outward, and she came with a force that left her clinging to Memphis in its wake.

* * *

Shoulder propped against the bathroom wall, Memphis silently watched Kate reapply her lipstick.

"My dress is creased," Kate said.

"No one will notice."

"And my hair is a mess," she said.

"You look fine."

She looked better than fine, she looked beautiful. And although the ice-princess persona was firmly back in place, he was beginning to recognize the signs of the underlying edginess brimming beneath her reserve.

Usually it was the subtle, rapid blinks of her eyelids that were the only clue to her distress. Right now it was evident in the faint tremble of her fingers as she swept a blond wisp of hair from her cheek and tucked it back into place. The strand had worked its way free from the elegant twist at the nape of her neck—most likely knocked loose when Memphis had held her head as Kate had worshipped his body with her mouth. The erotic memory brought an inevitable swell of desire, but Memphis pushed it aside. Because every tiny shake of her unsteady hands put another nick in his heart.

"The only thing anyone will notice is the glow in your face," Memphis said.

Kate pressed her palms to her cheeks, staring at her reflection in the mirror, her brow creased with concern. She'd spent most of her life so contained she probably wouldn't recognize her own feelings if they walked up and slapped her. He hadn't entered the bathroom to make love to her, only to tease and get a rise out of the normally composed woman.

Now he had an overwhelming urge to get her away from this toxic environment, to get her to *relax.*

"I'll take you home," he said

She met his gaze in the mirror. "I don't want to leave right away."

Surprised, Memphis shifted his weight on his feet. "I figured after everything the gossipmongers had said—"

"No," Kate said as she turned and leaned back against the bathroom counter, bracing her hands on the marble behind her. "I told you before, I don't care what they think about my marriage."

He tipped his head. "So what does Kate Anderson care about?"

Kate didn't hesitate. "Fixing my life."

The regal set to her chin disturbed him more than he wanted to admit. He folded his arms against his chest, hating that he had to ask the words out loud. "Does that include continuing to stay away from me?"

Her forehead crumpled in confusion. "I don't know, Memphis," she said, the doubt and the uncertainty and the honesty cutting deeper than they should. "I just don't know anymore."

The look on her face made his chest grow tight, and he pushed away from the wall. "Damn it, Kate," he said softly. Reaching the woman had never seemed so important, and he finally admitted to himself just how much was at stake. "Please tell me you're not engaged in some sort of self-torture mission because of what we did five years ago. As if you don't deserve pleasure or happiness because of the past." He hiked an eyebrow. "Because martyrdom isn't an attractive quality in this day and age."

Kate let out a small self-deprecating laugh. "If avoiding pleasure was my intent, I wouldn't be doing a very good job of it, now would I?"

Despite the tension, a smile tugged at the corner of his mouth. "Not really."

Her gaze shifted away from his. "And not that I think suffering in any way shape or form makes up for my sins, but trust me when I tell you I've suffered quite a bit already."

"How?"

Kate's expression went blank, and then she turned back to the sink. Not meeting his gaze in the mirror, she washed her hands, as if she hadn't washed them two times already.

"How?" he repeated.

She pulled a tissue from the decorative container on the counter and pivoted to face him, holding it out to him. Clearly she was stalling for time.

"What's that for?" he asked, refusing to take the tissue.

Kate nodded in his direction, not meeting his gaze. "I suggest you wipe your mouth. Mind you, you have testosterone to spare, but the lipstick really detracts from your manly appearance."

A muscle in his jaw ticked, not that he gave a damn about having Kate Anderson's lipstick coloring his mouth. Memphis shifted on his feet, refusing to budge. "What happened when you told Dalton about us?" he said

She blinked hard, and then turned back to the sink, rearranging the contents of a decorative basket on the counter. "All things considered, he took it remarkably well," she said, her tone carefully even. But the nervous activity of her hands was a dead giveaway. "He knew we were in trouble, and he acknowledged he was also at fault for the two of us drifting apart," she went on, her fingers smoothing the petal of a silk flower. "The competition to get into the law school he wanted was tough. And that meant his college years consisted of him being buried in the books. Spending hours away from home."

"Lots of couples survive similar circumstances."

Kate shook her head gently. "It got worse in law school, and even when he *was* home, he wasn't mentally with me."

Memphis knew there was more to the story, and he met her gaze in the mirror and, lifting an I'm-not-going-away brow, he said, "But what was his reaction about us?"

Kate heaved out a breath, and scrunched her eyes closed, her thumb and her forefinger pinching the bridge of her nose. "We talked about everything in depth with a marriage counselor, and Dalton seemed to come to grips with the news.

He was even able to discuss his feelings with the counselor in a logical, reasonable fashion. He told me he wanted to fix our marriage."

"So what was the problem, Kate?"

She dropped her hand to her side and met his gaze in the mirror. "At home he began to hurl indirect slurs my way."

He stared at her, as if he could will her not to look away.

"I couldn't discuss his humiliating words with any of my friends." She let out a low laugh that held no humor. "And I certainly didn't want to confess to my family what I'd done."

"Did you ask him to stop?" he said.

There was a small pause before she answered. "I did, but that only made his derisive comments worse," she said. "He started making them in public, too, trying to hide them behind humor. He told jokes about women being untrustworthy. Liars and cheats. The only one not laughing was me." She met his gaze again. "And the comments grew more vindictive as time went by." Kate swiped an imaginary hair from her cheek, as if trying to brush aside the unhappy memories. "Until I finally realized he just couldn't forgive me."

Memphis watched her smooth her hand down her dress, as if trying to fix the faint creases from their moment of passion, and Memphis couldn't take the nervous activity anymore. He reached out to wrap his fingers lightly around her wrist, subduing her antsy hand. He held her gaze, his voice low. "Four years is a long time to spend seeking forgiveness," he said, rubbing his thumb along the pounding pulse at the base of her thumb.

Her blue eyes were alive with emotion. "Especially when you're struggling to forgive yourself."

The words pinched his heart, and Memphis frowned. "Kate, you came clean. You tried to repair your marriage. There was nothing more you could have done." Kate didn't look convinced, and Memphis went on, struggling to convince her of the truth. "Ultimately," he said. "Dalton made his own choice."

Despite everything, a part of him had to ask the question, his gut tightening uneasily. "Do you still have feelings for him?"

Her sigh was so small it was almost inaudible. "I still believe in his politics. I know better than anyone that his commitment to serving the people is genuine." She lifted her chin, squarely meeting his gaze. "And I will always support him unconditionally in his fight to better the lives of others. But no," she said, shaking her head softly. "The only feelings that remain are the ones of respect for his dedication to his work."

An intense feeling of satisfaction bloomed. And suddenly, the need to leave the complications behind was intense. "I found a side door while searching for the den," he said. "I say we slip out and leave this party behind."

Kate's hesitation was brief. "On two conditions."

Doubt narrowed his eyes. "Which are…?"

"First, we fix your appearance." Kate reached up and wiped his mouth with the tissue, and Memphis was left wishing she'd used her lips instead. "Real men don't wear lipstick."

"And second?"

"You *have* to feed me."

As if on cue, her stomach growled, and a smile crept up his face. "Deal," he said. "I know the perfect place."

CHAPTER NINE

FROM the outside, the old fishing wharf restaurant looked as if it had fallen on hard times, but Memphis knew better. And the number of cars in the parking lot confirmed the unique establishment's popularity. As they made their way for the door, Memphis loosely linked his fingers with Kate's, enjoying the feel of skin on skin. And while there was nothing better than touching her in the midst of a round of passionate sex, he craved this simple contact, too.

"When you took me home to change into jeans," she said. "I thought we'd end up at a beachside dive with sand under my toes."

Chuckling, Memphis opened the door and led her inside. Music blared, people chatted loudly and mouthwatering smells filled the air. "*This* dive has the world's best hamburgers and a great selection of beers," he said. Just inside the doorway, Kate slipped her hand from his, and disappointment surged—because he missed her touch. "It also has a conspicuous lack of a judgmental public." He shot her a meaningful look as he steered her through the crowd. "When you decide to come to Rick's, you don't need to worry about a thing."

Kate took a seat at one of the large wooden cable spools that doubled as tables, and her lips twisted wryly. "Except, perhaps, getting a tetanus shot," she said dryly, eyeing the bar along the wall that was creatively fashioned out of wooden shipping crates.

Memphis chuckled as he sat in the chair beside her. "No nails, I promise," he said, patting the table, which had a clear coat finish.

A perky waitress arrived to take their order, and when she retreated, Memphis turned back to Kate. "I promise you, no one in here has noticed nor cares that you are Kate Anderson."

"No pitying looks for the ex–Mrs. Worthington?" she said lightly.

Memphis studied her face, but her relaxed expression matched her tone. Since they'd left the party, her tension had evaporated. Still, he knew that Tabitha's malicious words had disturbed Kate, and he felt the need to offer reassurance. "Tabitha Reed is a useless phony."

"She's been a thorn in my side since high school."

"I'm shocked." His lips quirked. "Don't you feel obligated to say nice things about her?"

She shot him a look. "That *was* me being nice."

"Ahhh," he said with a smile. "That was your delicate way of calling her a pain in the ass."

"Yes." She clearly was fighting a grin. "But she was good for one thing."

He hiked a skeptical eyebrow. "Defining the word *bitch?*"

Kate let out a laugh, and the sound rolled through him, warming his insides and delighting him more than it should. Her blue blouse brought out the color of her eyes and was casually youthful, not the political-wife style she usually wore. With her shoulder-length, wheat-colored hair framing her face, she looked younger than her twenty-eight years.

And the new lightness in her eyes was infectious.

"That, too." She folded her arms on the table. "But I was talking about her scathing appraisal of my life."

He winced on her behalf, and, overwhelmed with the need to offer comfort, he covered her palm with his. "Kate—"

As if acting reflexively, she gently pulled her hand away again, her soft skin slipping from his grasp. But, instead of her standard chastising look, she sent him a smile. Which was an improvement, but not as much as he would have liked. "While waiting in the bathroom for you to break up the gossip fest," she said. "I realized you and Tabitha were both right."

His brow crinkled with doubt. "She and I sure as hell never agreed on anything."

"You both claimed I didn't have a life outside of my marriage," she said. "And it's true."

Stunned by her words, he waited for her to go on, knowing the admission had to have been difficult. "I loved organizing the fundraiser functions," she said. "But ultimately, Dalton reaped the benefits, not me."

Pleased with her confession, he leaned his elbows on the unusual table. "So, what is Kate Anderson going to do now?"

"Something I thought about years ago. I'm going to start my own event-planning business."

Pleasure surged. "Good for you." He tipped his head curiously. "What stopped you before?"

"My parents encouraged me to wait until Dalton was more established in his career." She pursed her lips. "But I suspect they were just worried I'd fail."

His eyebrows shot up in surprise. "If anyone can make the business a success, it's you."

"Thanks," she said with a small laugh. "But in high school, Tabitha was the one voted most likely to succeed."

"And you were voted most popular."

As if unimpressed, Kate gave a tiny roll of her eyes. "Success is much more desirable than popularity."

Memphis let out a small scoff at the irony. "I've learned that the first can buy you the second." His lips quirked in humor. "Did you know I was recognized by my senior class, too?"

"And what notable title were you appointed?" she said, amusement shining in her eyes. "Best killer smile? Most likely to bring a woman to her knees?"

Memories of the bathroom hit, and desire surged in response. "You know how much I love it when you're on your knees," he murmured.

Instantly her gaze grew dark, her throaty tone confirming her sensual gaze. "Careful, Memphis." Folding her arms on the table again, she leaned in, the proximity increasing the feeling of seclusion. "That comes dangerously close to male chauvinism."

"If it's any consolation..." He held her gaze, more than pleased with the sense of intimacy. "I won the most insane vote."

"Fitting," she said softly. "Which crazy event earned you that title?"

"Right after your senior prom, I dived off the Biscayne Bridge. It was a great way to rid myself of a little sexual frustration."

Her brows rose curiously. "If you spent most of my prom in the parking lot with Tiffany Bettingfield, where does the sexual frustration come into play?"

He took her hand, expecting her to resist again. Instead, Kate laced her fingers with his, her heated gaze and the small success thrilling Memphis to the core. Memory, and the soft, promising contact set his body on fire. "She wasn't you."

The scorching look that passed through his sinfully sexy eyes sent a heated flush surging through Kate's body. Holding his hand felt almost decadent, and her heart thudded so hard there was no room in her chest to breathe. But she couldn't have pulled away again, even if she'd wanted to.

After several moments filled with a mutual desire, his gaze intense, Memphis said, "Where are we going from here, Kate?"

Kate stared at him, trying to process his question, knowing he was referring to their relationship. As the internal war was fought over what to do next, she lifted her gaze to his gorgeously mussed brown hair. And this time she had firsthand knowledge that it was the work of her fingers. Palm pressed against his, she subdued the urge to smooth his hair with her other hand, frightened by the tender feelings that the image brought.

Before she could resolve the battle being fought in her head, Memphis went on. "I get that you don't want to add any more fuel to the gossipmongers. And clearly, going public with any kind of relationship, outside of a friendship, will do just that." His fingers curled more firmly around hers, and she basked in the electric sensation. "But I won't allow you to continue to pretend the chemistry between us is because you've gone so long without sex."

She licked her suddenly parched lips. "I—"

"Because it isn't."

Her shoulders drooped a bit, giving in to the weight of the overwhelming truth. "I know."

He didn't give her a chance to continue, his

voice low and determined. "From now on, until this reunion is over, if I want to take you to bed I will." A thrill shot through her. He rubbed her palm with his thumb, sending a potent shimmer of desire straight between her legs. Her now weak and *shaky* legs. "Hell," he said. "If I want to sleep with you every night between now and the final party, I will." He paused, as if letting the statement fully sink in before going on. "Do you understand what I'm saying?"

As the sultry tension edged higher, she stared at him. He wasn't trying to intimidate her. He wasn't being a tyrant. He was simply a man who had reached the end of his patience.

"I understand," she said.

He paused, as if expecting to hear an argument. When none came, he said, "So, do you agree to my conditions?"

Kate blinked once. Hard. She could refuse his demands, and that would be the end. Memphis would walk away and never look back. And although she'd come to terms with her mistakes long ago, she'd finally accepted that nothing she did now could ever undo what she'd done back then, either, which was a huge step forward to taking back her life.

Memphis would eventually leave town in search of the next big stunt, she accepted that inevitable truth. But for the first time in years the end of the day would be something to look forward to. And it was about more than great sex. It was the laughter, the *companionship*. She couldn't bear the thought of missing out on this chance.

She'd wanted to be with Memphis since she was a teen, and, right or wrong, she was done pretending she didn't. "Agreed," she said.

His thumb went still, and his gaze grew impossibly black, as if someone had poured melted dark chocolate into a glass full of whiskey.

A hamburger platter appeared on the table before her, a tantalizing smell reaching her nose, and Kate blinked in surprise, looking up at the young waiter responsible for the intrusion. He was dressed in baggy pants, a T-shirt and an eager expression.

Her expression probably reflected her desperation and pounding heart. Neither of which had anything to do with the arrival of food and everything to do with the way Memphis was looking at her—as if he was ready to drag her into the nearest bathroom.

"Enjoy your meal," the waiter said, placing a matching plate in front of Memphis. Instead of leaving them to their dinner, the guy turned to Memphis. "I took up BASE jumping three years ago. I'm a big fan of your work."

Memphis maintained his hold on Kate's hand. "Thanks," he said to the waiter.

The man assumed a relaxed posture, as if ready for a long discussion. "I was at the New River Gorge the year you and that Anderson guy made a simultaneous double gainer BASE jump."

Memphis shot the waiter a genuine smile. "That was a good one."

"It was a *beauty*," the waiter said with enthusiasm. "I was stoked for days after." And then his face scrunched lightly, as if trying to remember. "And wasn't the jump you two did from the top of the Anderson office building the one that injured your friend?"

At the resurrection of the awful memories, Kate's heart sputtered to a stop, and Memphis's thumb on her palm went still, the pleasant expression wiped from his face.

Tension tightened in the air, but the BASE-jumping waiter was oblivious as he went on. "I hear he almost died. Is he walking better now?"

The clatter of dishes, chattering guests and music filled the pause, the waiter clearly expecting a response, but it was Kate who recovered first. "Brian Anderson is doing just fine," she said with a strained smile.

Memphis cleared his throat and pulled his hand from Kate's. "Yeah," he muttered. "He's great. Thanks for the food."

As the waiter retreated, Memphis started to eat, avoiding her gaze. Heart pumping at the reminder of another awkward part of their past, Kate shifted her eyes to her meal, no longer hungry...and missing the feel of Memphis's hand on hers.

Two days later, Kate gripped her iced tea and tried to enjoy the sunny, bird's-eye view of Miami from the rooftop bar of the Anderson Towers—the perfect mix of elegant decor and a relaxed, Sunday-afternoon attitude. Earlier she'd been finishing up brunch with her family at the Country Club when Memphis had called and asked her to meet him here. After forty-eight hours of silence she'd been grateful for the contact. She'd also been grateful for a break from defending her choice of a date to her parents. They were unhappy to hear she considered Memphis a friend. Imagine how disappointed they'd be to know he was so much more? Or at least, he *used* to be more.

After the disastrous reminder of reality at dinner, Kate was no longer sure.

The conversation had been strained as they'd eaten their meal at Rick's. Memphis had been quiet, almost withdrawn, and she'd been lost in the horrible memories of Brian's accident—and all the things she'd said to Memphis that day....

Her stomach rolled, and Kate pressed a palm to her belly. When Memphis appeared on the rooftop deck, she gave up her efforts at self-comfort.

Because, although the office building was part of her family's extensive holdings, he strolled onto the teak deck as if he owned the place, seizing her immediate attention. The athletic grace. The easy, yet commanding attitude. In jeans and a snug T-shirt, every muscle was lovingly emphasized, and he had a small backpack slung over one shoulder.

But of all the possible locales, why had Memphis wanted to meet her here?

She knew the answer had to do with Brian's accident. Hating the barrier between them, she realized it was time to address this painful part of their history. Searching for a way to start the conversation as he drew closer, Kate said, "Most people come to Miami to enjoy the view of the ocean, not the tops of skyscrapers."

Memphis ignored the subtle inquiry. He signaled the waitress and ordered a drink before dropping into a seat at the table, setting his pack next to his feet. "I'm not most people, Kate."

No, he definitely wasn't.

The whiskey-colored, thickly fringed eyes oozed the usual sex appeal, but there was a subtle hardness that had been there since the waiter had mentioned the accident. She scanned his face wondering what was going through his mind, and she remembered her brother's warning words. Memphis wouldn't be around much longer. And time was running out.

Fear squeezed her chest, an emotion she'd refused to acknowledge until now. Intuitively, she realized this was the reason why she'd dreaded asking Memphis for help.

When he was around, her heart was at its most vulnerable.

The waitress returned with his drink and then retreated, and Memphis drawled, "How are good ol' Mom and Dad?"

She kept her tone light. "As well as ever, thanks for asking."

His mouth twitched with amusement. "Still rich?"

She steadily met his gaze. "Richer," she said. "That's the thing about making smart financial decisions. Money seems to grow as a result."

"My parents would say being smart doesn't help if you have no money to invest." There was no bitterness in his tone. "Did my name come up at the Country Club?"

"No," she said, swallowing hard after the lie. She carefully set her glass down, and continued with the truth. "We discussed Dad's retirement. This next election will be his last."

"Good thing he stuck around long enough to get your ex elected."

She shot him a pointed look. "He wasn't my ex during the last election."

"Oh, yeah," he said, as if he'd just remembered. But she knew it was just for show. "You two were pretending to be the happily married couple while you were locked away in your chastity tower..." He paused, his eyes gleaming with an amused light. "Taking care of yourself," he added with emphasis.

She held his gaze, resisting the urge to roll her eyes, her eyebrow lifting a touch. "There are advantages to not sharing a bedroom with a man."

"And what would those be?" Eyes creased with humor, he crossed his arms, the biceps stretching his shirt. The resultant tug of female appreciation momentarily made it a struggle to remember.

"No middle-of-the-night, unpleasant discovery that the toilet seat has been left up," she said. "No dirty socks littering the floor."

His lips twitched. "Is that all?"

Kate shot him a pointed look. "No dealing with a man who refuses to return your call."

She'd known he'd needed time to recover from the waiter's remark, so she'd tried hard not to be hurt during his two days of silence. But Memphis obviously had no intention of sharing what was going on in his mind. And, as she steadily held his gaze, the moment stretched to the point of discomfort, until a waiter dropped by to refill her iced tea, eyeing Memphis curiously, as if recognizing his face but not placing the name.

When their tête-à-tête had been restored, she said, "I think he wanted to ask if you were Memphis James." She studied him for a moment. "Does the publicity bother you?"

Furrows of subdued humor appeared on his forehead. "The problem with being in the public light is that I'm never sure if people are being nice because they want something from me or not." He didn't sound resentful, only vaguely amused. He briefly turned his gaze to the city skyline. "Which makes me wary of every friendship. At least with Brian I always know exactly where I stand."

A gentle prompting seemed in order. "You wouldn't know it by your visits back home," she said as lightly as she could. "You hardly ever come back." When he didn't respond, she leaned forward, searching his eyes, needing to tackle the wall between them. "Memphis, about Brian's accident—"

"Do you remember what you said to me that day?" He tipped his head, ignoring her words. The pressure in her chest grew uncomfortable. "You told me you hated me and never wanted to see me again," he said.

Her quoted statement smacked her full-on, and Kate closed her eyes, the fear and the anger and the sorrow coming back. The days following Brian's accident had been the worst of her life. When she lifted her lids, she met his gaze. "I didn't mean it."

But Memphis had left Miami anyway, and she hadn't seen him again until his recent return to town.

He tipped his head skeptically, his lips quirking at the edges. "Your words sounded heartfelt at the time."

"I was upset. The statement just slipped from my mouth."

The doubtful look he shot her was still filled with skeptical humor. "Was it an accident when you shoved me out the door of the hospital waiting room?"

"It was a stressful time, Memphis," she said, the horrible pressure in her chest increasing. "Brian was hurt, and we were dealing with the news he might not survive the brain swelling from his head injury. My parents were falling apart. And they needed me to be strong." Heart frantically beating, she didn't stop to catch her breath. "They were so angry at you about the accident, and I had just gone back to Dalton after you and I had…"

When she didn't continue, he lifted an eyebrow, as if daring her to go on.

And if she'd hoped he would make it easier by filling in the blank for her, she should have known better. "Can't you say the words?" he said.

"Slept together," she finally finished.

"You never told your family about that night."

It wasn't a question, and she was sure Memphis didn't expect her to answer, but she tried anyway. "I don't think it would have gone over well," she said, wincing at the understatement.

Memphis let out a low chuckle that lacked much amusement. "I don't suppose it would have."

"Look," she said seriously. "You and I both know it would have made a bad situation worse," she said. "Brian needed to focus on recovery. And my parents…" Words failed her again so she left it at a helpless shrug.

"Would have had a cow," Memphis said dryly.

Despite everything, she smiled at her old expression from childhood. "They would have had a whole herd."

"Yeah," he said. "I don't think they could have handled learning you were human at the same time their only son was seriously injured."

"My parents are well aware that I'm human."

"Are they?" he said, narrowing his eyes in doubt. The reservation on his face was real. "Sometimes I'm not so sure." He crossed his arms on the table. "You didn't struggle with their expectations like Brian did; being a royal Anderson came easy to you. But he hated the pressure your parents placed on him to conform." He sent her a look that eased a bit of the tension in her belly. "When we first met, he was looking to push the boundaries and I was an out-of-control kid looking for trouble."

"The dynamic duo was a pretty lethal combination." Despite her tension, a smile tugged at the corner of her mouth. "Most of the time I didn't know who infuriated me more. Brian," she said. "Or you."

"Which was always half the fun of any stunt we pulled." He leaned back in his seat, his eyes amused. "Did Brian ever tell you we used to take bets as to which expression would come out of your mouth when you'd hunt us down?"

"No," she said, leaning forward curiously. "He never said a word."

A sound of amusement escaped his lips. "You Andersons are way too secretive."

She ignored his statement. "So what were the reprimanding phrases I used again?"

"'Dad's ready to blow his top, Brian,'" he said, and Kate had to laugh at his lousy job at imitating her voice. "Or the old standby that was usually directed at me, 'How could you be so stupid?'

But my personal favorite involved your warning there was an imminent bovine delivery at the Anderson house." The grin on his face grew bigger. "You know," he said, his smile grew wistful. "My family was dirt-poor, but those years were the happiest times of my life."

The confession surprised her. "Better than now?"

"In some ways." His smile turned cynical. "But certainly not all."

"What do you miss the most?"

He looked out over the city, the words soft. "I miss the days of planning stunts with Brian."

Her fingers stilled on her glass, and she waited for Memphis to go on. He squinted, as if to block the bright sunshine limiting his view of the city. She sensed the weight of his guilt about the accident, blaming himself.

Well, Kate. That might have something to do with the fact that you told *him he was to blame.*

She gripped her iced tea, remembering more of her awful, painful words the day she'd pushed Memphis out of the hospital waiting room, scared her parents would exit Brian's room and find him there. Scared of the turbulent scene that would surely follow. Her parents were distraught, livid and they would have certainly taken the emotions out on Memphis.

Memphis clearly didn't want to discuss her old accusation, but she had to try again. "It's not your fault," she said.

This time his scoff was infused with denial.

"Brian chose your family's building for the jump because he knew it would piss your parents off the most. But *I* chose the day with the unfavorable wind conditions."

She reached out to touch his arm. "Memphis," she said. "We really need to talk—"

The words died when he removed his arm from her hand and pulled out his wallet, tossing a large bill on the table. The amount more than covered their two drinks and a generous tip.

"I've got to go, Kate," he said as he reached down and slid both arms into his backpack. It was then she noticed a smaller bag attached with a cord.

This was no ordinary backpack.

"Memphis," she said. The hairs on the back of her neck stood up, and the warning that had been buzzing in the back of her brain since he'd first asked to meet her here, of all places, grew louder. "What are you doing?"

He stood, backpack now securely strapped to his back, the smaller bag in his hand. And the grin he sent her was full of mischief. One she knew far too well.

"Taking the fastest way down," he said.

A low strangled sound escaped her lips. "Memphis James," she said. She shot to her feet and followed him as he started to jog toward the railing, her voice growing louder, increasing her pace even as her throat closed over, squeezing her heart. "Don't you dare—"

Without pause, or fear or any sign of a second thought, Memphis nimbly vaulted over the rail.

Kate gasped and reached the rail just as the bartender let out a shout, and several of the patrons rushed to join Kate. There was a one-second pause of shocked silence, until Memphis's falling form threw up the smaller pack, a tiny parachute opening, pulling out a bigger one which caught the air with a whoosh, abruptly slowing Memphis's descent. Loud whoops of cheers and relieved laughter came from the guests. The smattering of applause and whistles were clearly ones of approval, and Kate bit back the frown, hoping Memphis couldn't hear.

As if the infuriating man needed any encouragement.

Kate gripped the rail, her whole body throbbing from the adrenaline as she watched him glide gracefully through the air toward the empty lot far below. She didn't breathe again until he landed and she was sure he wasn't dead.

Which was great, because now she was going to hunt him down and throttle him herself.

CHAPTER TEN

It took Kate longer to show up at his apartment than Memphis had expected. After enjoying the peaceful sound of rushing air, he'd landed, quickly gathered his chute and hopped into his car parked by the empty lot—making a fast getaway before the cops arrived. And it was a full twenty minutes after he entered his apartment before he heard the inevitable pounding on his door, and his lips twisted wryly.

He opened the door to the beautiful sight of Kate's face, flushed with fury, her delicious body elegantly attired in the light pink sundress that probably cost more than his father had made in a month.

"Memphis Nathanial James," she bit out, hands on her hips. "If you ever pull a stunt like that again, you won't need to continue to court death for a living, because I will kill you myself."

"Hmm," he said, his lips quirking as he stepped back and held the door open. "Though I miss the birthing a cow reference, I like the sassier new reprimand."

She brushed past him, leaving a trail of lavender-scented air. "What the *hell* did you think you were doing?"

He closed the door. "That's hardly appropriate language for a representative's spouse."

"I am not a representative's spouse anymore."

"I don't think Senator Anderson and his wife would approve of you cussing, either."

She came to a stop in his living room and whirled to face him. "Memphis," she said. For a moment she looked as if she would stamp her foot in frustration. "I don't care if my parents approve or not."

His mouth twisted at the irony. "Well, there's a first," he said, the sarcasm oozing out before he could stop it.

There was a two-second pause before she said, "Why do you insist on antagonizing them?"

For a moment, the question stumped him. "What are you talking about?"

"You know my parents will hear about the jump. You *know* they'll figure out it was you." She stepped closer, her blue eyes snapping. But her expression was more about a woman trying to figure out a puzzle, and growing exasperated that she couldn't. "Why do you go out of your way to make things difficult?"

A tiny seed of anger formed in his chest. "This might be a bit of a stretch for you to understand, but my decisions are based on *my* needs, not those of the almighty Anderson family. And if they don't approve, then that's too bad."

"I just spent brunch trying to explain to my parents how *nice* you were to accompany me to the reunion."

"Why would you bother?" he said. He cocked his head, holding her gaze. "And I thought you said my name didn't come up."

She blinked twice before responding. "I...I lied."

"You do that a lot."

For a moment, Kate looked at a loss for words, and Memphis decided to help her out.

Not that she would appreciate his efforts.

"So who brought up the subject of Memphis James? You?" he said, knowing the question was absurd. "Or your parents?"

She pressed her lips together for a moment. "Tabitha told my mother you came with me to the party."

Damn, he hated being right. He digested the news, wondering how the cool little princess had managed the conversation with her parents. No doubt with finesse and grace, like always.

He knew the answer, but he had to ask anyway. "Did you tell them you were involved with me?"

She heaved out a breath. "Of course not," she said.

The bark of laughter that broke from his throat was bitter, and Kate pressed her fingers to her temples, as if trying to keep her head from exploding.

After a silence-filled moment, she dropped her hand to her side. "Memphis," she said, clearly struggling for patience. "My parents loved Dalton. They doted on him and were as active in his political campaign as anyone else. *More* so. The publicity from the divorce has been hard on them too. I'm just—" She stopped and inhaled slowly, as if she wanted to hold it together but was suddenly too weary from all the effort. "I'm just trying to keep things as calm as possible."

He refused to release her gaze. "Because we both know you don't like it when things get difficult."

Kate's mouth dropped open, as if on the verge of a dispute. But then both her lips and her lids closed. Whatever she'd been about to say, she wiped the anger from her face, choosing a different question. Finally, she opened her eyes, her voice resigned as she said softly, "What do you want from me?"

And the answer came roaring into his head.

Anything. *Everything.*

But that was one truth he would never utter out loud.

He slowly shook his head, feeling a little wiped out himself. "Nothing, Kate," he said as he turned to face his living-room window, staring down at the Miami street below. Why had he come back to this town again? "Nothing at all."

There was a long pause, and then Kate spoke from behind. "That's not what you said at the restaurant."

Desire stabbed him in the gut, the force so powerful it hurt to breathe.

"If I remember right," she went on. "You said if you wanted to sleep with me every night between now and the reunion you would."

"I remember what I said."

"It's been two nights now."

Need coiled tightly in his gut. He didn't respond, just stared down at the cars on the road and tried to ignore the woman who was driving him insane, his heart pounding out a crazy rhythm.

When he didn't reply, she tried again, as if searching for what was bothering him. "Way back when, I had to go back to Dalton," she said quietly, and his chest pinched his lungs. "I couldn't have lived with myself, especially after what I'd done, unless I tried everything within my power to fix my marriage."

He dragged in a breath. Deep down he'd known the truth. He'd *always* known. Not that it had made it any easier.

"It's okay, Kate," he said. "I understand."

But it was hard as hell being the one left behind. And as he continued to stare down at the street, he finally realized Kate didn't have to walk away to cause him pain. She was doing a mighty fine job in person.

"I've always wanted you, Memphis," she went on softly, the words curling in his chest, expanding, taking up more room than they should. Threatening to overwhelm his every thought. "Even as a teen. Even as you and Brian used to antagonize my parents with your hell-raising antics. Even as you used to tease me and drive me nuts." Memphis turned to face her, taking in her steady gaze. The frank honesty on her face. "You were big and you were bold and you were so beautiful I couldn't take my eyes off you," she said, and desire licked at his body. "I just didn't want you to know."

His voice was rough. "I knew."

And it was immensely unsatisfying to suffer through an intense attraction when the other person seemed damn determined to pretend it didn't exist. He'd always wondered if the wanting but not having was what had made her like a drug he couldn't quit.

Unfortunately, now he knew it wasn't true.

He wanted to pull her into his arms. But he'd waited years to hear this confession and he wasn't going to touch her until she finished.

"I'm sure you could sense it," she went on. "Even as I was yelling at you and Brian for pulling a stupid stunt."

"You were frustrated."

Her laugh was shaky. "I was so hot for you I didn't know which way was up."

The words escaped before he could corral them. "You were damn good at hiding your feelings," he said. "Every time you lifted your chin and shot me that cool, disapproving expression I wanted to jerk you into my arms and kiss the reserved look right out of your eyes. And then when I approached you at your prom, to say congratulations, you looked right past me." He let out a soft snort of old anger, the self-mocking smile easing it a touch. "I was so ticked off at you."

She sent him a sad smile. "If it's any consolation, I knew exactly when you and Tiffany went to your car." Her beautiful lips quirked, but he couldn't tell if it was from amusement or sadness. "There I was with Dalton. A charming, smart and handsome guy a person couldn't help but love, and that included me and my parents." She met his gaze again, her voice clear, the years of longing evident in her troubled eyes. "But I couldn't stop wondering what it would be like to be the one in your backseat."

With a crude curse, Memphis hauled her against his chest, letting loose the bottled-up energy via a scalding kiss.

He didn't bother with finesse as he speared his fingers into her hair, knocking the pins loose, the strands falling free, angling her head to take her mouth with all the pent-up sexual urges and resentment he'd felt in his teens. Problem was, the mountain of discontent from those years was too large to be so easily leveled.

He attempted anyway, the kiss turning raw, his mouth trying to merge with hers, his teeth intermittently nipping at her lower lip, his tongue subduing hers into a dance he led with a vengeance. And she kissed him back.

This wasn't about her years of going without sex. This wasn't about just the crackling electricity that burned whenever they were in the same room. This was about the frustrating teenage years they'd endured. And the hormonally driven angst of wanting and not having.

As if sensing the extent of his need, Kate didn't try to direct the moment, simply going along with whatever he wanted, whenever he wanted to do it. She returned his kiss with, if not total submission, at least with a concession that right here, right now, Memphis James owned Kate Anderson.

It was Memphis who shucked his clothes and tossed them aside.

It was Memphis who unzipped her dress and pushed it and her panties to the floor.

And when Kate's hands shifted to his hips, as if to pull him close, Memphis gruffly muttered something even he didn't understand and grabbed her wrists, pinning them at her sides. The desire to consume every inch of her, to stamp his claim on Kate, left no room for subtlety. His lips worked their way down her body, an open-mouthed, hungry kiss over the pounding pulse at her throat, a soft scrape of his teeth across the tantalizing tip of her breast, thrilling at the sounds coming from Kate. With the scent of lavender in his nose, the salty, silken skin of her abdomen on his tongue, he knelt in front of her.

His voice rough, he gave a single command. "Kate."

And she complied, parting her legs.

His mouth tasted, his tongue teased and the choked sounds of pleasure coming from Kate's mouth brought him immense satisfaction. When he couldn't wait any longer, he stood and lifted her up, and she wrapped her legs around his waist as he carried her into the corridor. She buried her face in his neck, her warm breath coming quick, but she said nothing as he strode down the hallway and, with a small kick, pushed open the door to his room.

Never letting her hips go, he planted a knee on his mattress and laid her back on the bed, moving over her and into her with a sure thrust of his hips.

Kate bowed her body, arching her back.

He laced his fingers through hers. Pressing her hands above her head, he repeatedly and relentlessly rocked his hips with the force of a passion born of the years of denial: every surreptitious look from their teens, every cool slide of her gaze to somewhere over his shoulder, and every heated argument that he now knew, in part, was born of sexual frustration. For every one of those moments his hard length drove deep between her legs, seeking more of the softness—as if to confirm that, yes, he hadn't been alone in the wanting. And though he led the wild, reckless pace, Kate followed willingly, meeting him thrust for thrust.

The promise of deep pleasure tightened low in his back, the age-old ache devouring him from the inside out, and he lifted his head to look down at the beautiful face he'd fantasized about in his youth. Cheeks flushed, her blue eyes smoky, she was close to orgasm, he could tell. And when she arched her neck, her lips red from his rough kisses, his name spilled from her mouth as she called out her completion, and his need became acute.

The torturous burn low in his back became a raging fire. Pushing him further. Driving him higher. Until the height of pleasure grew so great that, with a final thrust, he took the greatest highfall of his life.

As their overheated bodies cooled, Kate listened to Memphis's heart slowly recover, her cheek resting on his hard chest. Her muscles slack, her limbs loose, she basked in the afterglow of their explosion, her fingers tracing the scar on his collarbone. She didn't care that her body was damp from the exertion. She didn't care her hair was so tangled it would take a shower and a whole bottle of conditioner to comb it out. All she felt was a bone-deep contentment.

But she needed to finish the conversation he had avoided on the roof of her family's building.

She stared at the far wall, gathering her courage. "I didn't mean it."

Memphis's arms tightened around her back, and he gave a sleepy "hmm" as his legs shifted slightly against her.

"When we were at the hospital," she said, her words low, careful. "I didn't mean it when I said Brian's accident was your fault."

His chest stilled, as if he'd stopped breathing, and his arms tensed, the small movement barely perceptible. But the stillness and the silence in the room matched the coiled tension in his body, as if he were remembering that moment so many years ago. For a second she wondered if he was going to pretend he was asleep.

She swallowed hard, her hand curling against his chest, and she lifted her head, propping her chin on her fist.

He was staring up at the ceiling.

"Say something," she said.

One hand around her waist, he folded the other beneath his head as he dropped his gaze to hers. His expression was impassive, but she sensed he was gearing up to disagree with her.

In an effort to lighten the mood, she lifted a brow teasingly. "At least promise me you won't jump out the window to avoid the conversation."

"We're a wimpy two stories up." One half of his mouth eased into a position of humor. "Where's the fun in that?"

Relieved he wasn't retreating, she softened her expression, her brow crinkling in amusement. "It's a challenge when you don't have a parachute."

"There's a line of bushes beneath the window."

Her brows pulled together in shocked doubt. "How does that keep you from breaking your neck?"

"I've done it before. You just have to know how to fall," he said. She stared at him in disbelief as he sent her a half smile, pushing a tangled strand of hair from her cheek. "Don't worry, nowadays I land better jobs with state-of-the-art equipment."

She narrowed her eyes at him in suspicion. "I don't want to hear about the early days of your work, do I?"

"No, you don't," he said. As if he sensed her discomfort, he went on, clearly amused she was worried. "Look, Kate. I'm good at what I do. It's the one area of my life where I'm just as meticulous as you," he said.

And then the faint humor melted from his face, replaced by one that looked pained. He dropped his gaze to his fingers as he reached out to absently rub a tangled lock of her hair. "I should have called the jump that day, but I didn't," he said, his tone low, and her heart stalled in her chest. "I checked the wind speed and knew it was too much, but I didn't call the jump. Anything above five mph increases the risk."

Though the ache in his voice was heartbreaking, she was relieved he was at least willing to discuss the accident.

"It's not your fault," she said again.

Memphis let out a sharp scoff. "Yes, it is. Brian chose the location, but I'm the one who insisted on taking the jump that day. I'm the reason my best friend almost died, almost lost the ability to walk. Not to mention the limp it left him with…"

"You couldn't have known. And Brian doesn't blame you."

"How do you know?" he said, his voice strained. "Have you discussed it with him?"

She slowly drew in a breath. "No," she said. "By the time he was well enough to hold a discussion, it hardly mattered anymore."

He raised a skeptical brow. "So how do you know what he thinks?"

She steadily held his gaze. "I know he misses you."

The fingers on her hair grew still, and Memphis's gaze grew unfocused, as if lost in memory. "No matter what your parents thought of me, Brian always treated me like an equal," Memphis said. "He always treated me with respect."

"You're the only brother he ever had," Kate said, the emotion clogging her throat. His arm tightened around her waist, but he said nothing, so she tried again. "Just talk to him about it, Memphis."

"Maybe," he said, but his tone wasn't encouraging.

She shifted higher on his chest, forcing him to meet her gaze. "Promise me you will."

His whiskey eyes grew dark, and his hand left her hair for her hip. Her breath hitched in her throat, and breathing became difficult. Which got worse when the hard muscles of his thigh slid into a more intimate position between her legs, shifting her higher, her sensitive breasts rubbing against his chest.

His voice rumbled. "I'll think it about tomorrow," he said. And he threaded his fingers through her messy hair and brought her mouth to his.

She'd worry about the tangles later.

Five days later Kate was scanning the main ballroom of the Grand Royal Beach Club when Memphis murmured from behind, "Please tell me you wore that dress for me."

Heat surged, and a smile threatened. "Who else?" she said, forcing herself to keep her eyes forward.

The vast room was adorned in black and white, complete with candlelight, exotic fresh flowers and swaths of white satin gracing the ceiling. Reunion guests were trickling in, and after months of planning, a bit of nerves was to be expected. Instead, the red cocktail dress made her feel beautiful, sexy and ready for anything. Which was fitting, because Memphis made her feel exactly the same way. After almost a week of spending her nights with Memphis and her days planning her new business venture and preparing for the reunion, she should feel exhausted. All she felt was exhilarated.

Which made her doubly sad Memphis would eventually leave.

A sharp pang twisted her heart, but she pushed it aside. "If one more person asks me when Dalton will show up I'm going to scream."

"I suppose I should be worried you chose that outfit in order to make your ex jealous."

Kate lifted her eyes heavenward, because there

wasn't the tiniest trace of concern in his voice, mostly because the man knew he had nothing to worry about. When it came to commanding a woman's attention, Memphis James was second to no one.

"Or maybe you wore that dress to outshine your replacement," Memphis said.

Kate shot Memphis a look over her shoulder. "When they do finally show up, would you please not call her that to her face?"

"Would you prefer me to call her the soon-to-be new Mrs. Dalton Worthington?" he said. "Or perhaps your ex-husband's future ex-wife?"

Kate bit back the smile lest she encourage him further. "How about we just call her Olivia, since that's her name?" she said smoothly, finally turning to face him.

And just like every time she took in his form, she struggled to keep her eyes from devouring Memphis. In a T-shirt and jeans, he sapped the strength from her knees. In a custom-tailored black suit he was devastating. He was still the bold, impossible-to-predict stuntman, and the beautiful clothes failed to tame the whiskey-colored bedroom eyes and the sexily mussed brown hair. She blinked hard, trying to focus.

"Well," he drawled, skimming his eyes down her form. "Whatever she's called, there isn't a chance in hell she'll compare to you."

Pleasure bloomed in her chest. "Thank you," she said. "I'll admit it's refreshing *not* to be required to don the conservative political attire."

"What are the requirements?"

"To blend in as tastefully as possible," she said, smoothing a hand down the silk covering her hip. "So the bright red coloring of my dress would have been a bit of a risk."

"Hmm," he said, the deep rumble skittering along her spine. "Too bad, because I love risk."

"You don't just love it," she said dryly. "You live it."

And, as predicted, her parents had voiced their intense displeasure over Memphis's leap off the Anderson Tower office building. Technically she was their youngest offspring by a good two minutes, but her middle-child peacemaker skills had been given a real workout.

"If you're not taking risks, you're not living," he said, shifting closer. "And I'm pushing the envelope tonight. Because if I'd known what you were going to wear to unveil your bold new look, I wouldn't have agreed to continue to pretend to be just your brother's best friend. Clearly you're taking your new role outside the political realm seriously. You're not trying to blend in at all."

Although the pleated bodice and fitted waist of the sleeveless dress were tasteful and elegant, it was her first real foray into daring. "The plunging neckline would have been a real no-no," she said.

His eyes briefly landed on her breasts, sending a shimmer down her spine that immediately spread deliciously to more sensitive parts. "Makes me doubly glad I'm not in politics," he murmured.

Kate laughed. "No campaign advisor in their right mind would take you on."

He tipped his head. "I bet the elegantly cool Kate Anderson was a campaign advisor's dream."

"The deep V in the back of this dress would have sent Dalton's advisor into a tizzy."

"Interesting," Memphis murmured. He stepped closer and skimmed his hand across the bare skin of her back. "It's having a similar effect on me now."

The warmth of his palm and the memories it stirred momentarily interfered with her ability to breathe. But she still had a job to do. "I have to check in with security now," she said with real regret. "I don't want any members of the media crashing the event. The last thing I need is to have them trailing me trying to get a picture with me, Dalton and his fiancée."

Hand on her back, Memphis leaned in way too close, his rumbling voice creating goose bumps down her neck. "Wouldn't matter if they did," he said. "No one would see anything beyond you." He straightened, his heated gaze scuttling her thoughts, and Kate tried to remember what task she'd been about to do. Fortunately, Memphis reminded her. "Come find me when you're done speaking with security."

CHAPTER ELEVEN

THE large ballroom was the picture of posh—no tacky disco balls, crepe streamers or balloons for the graduates of Biscayne Bay Preparatory Academy. And while Memphis was perfectly comfortable in the surroundings, he was grateful to finally find Brian in the smaller adjoining reception room, the walls plastered with memorabilia and photos from ten years ago.

When Brian spied Memphis approaching, a spark lit his friend's eyes. "I saw the little blurb in the news about someone taking a leap off of the Anderson Tower." Brian's gaze twinkled with amusement. "There was a suggestion the jumper might have been you."

"All speculation."

"You caused quite a stir."

"It was a slow news day," Memphis said.

Of course, the media had dwelled more on his poverty-stricken childhood in Miami and the fateful accident than on Memphis's current success. His lips twisted at the irony. He'd come back to town wondering if time would have changed anything.

Apparently, not by much.

"I know most of the members of the reunion committee," Brian said as he lifted his beer in the direction a picture a little farther down the wall. "So I'm surprised that photo of the two of us survived the cut."

Memphis bit back a smile. "I suspect your sister used her considerable power as chairperson to override any objections that cropped up."

Brian held Memphis's gaze over his beer bottle. "It's probably a hint she'd like to have you around more." A muscle around Memphis's eye twitched at his tone, and Brian took a swig of his beer, the moment lingering as if he was waiting for Memphis to comment. When he didn't, Brian went on. "We could really use your expertise on the TV show," he said. "I'd make you an offer you couldn't refuse."

The question tunneled deep into his chest. Memphis hadn't wanted to come back to his old hometown and he sure as hell didn't want to give up his professional goals, especially given how little his reputation had changed in this city. But his time with Brian had been good, not to mention his time with Kate....

But technically they weren't even dating. Just working on satisfying years of longing while pretending in public—or trying to, anyway—that they were just friends. The conditions that had seemed reasonable in the beginning now left him with a vague sense of growing dissatisfaction.

"I appreciate the offer, Brian," he finally said. "But settling in one place doesn't fit with my long-term plans. And you know how it is. This isn't a nine-to-five profession. If someone calls, I go. The job takes me all over the world."

Brian gave a light shrug, but his tone was full of meaning. "It doesn't have to."

Fighting the pleasure the thought of staying brought, Memphis moved farther along the wall of photos, coming to a stop at the picture of the two of them. It'd been taken on a day Memphis had traveled across town to visit Brian after school. They were both wearing dirt-bike apparel and a considerable amount of dust from a vacant lot by Biscayne Bay Preparatory Academy—a parcel of land that had long since been replaced by a strip mall. A pang of nostalgia swept through Memphis, not for the loss of the lot but for a time when things were simpler. Less complicated.

And a hell of a lot clearer.

"Man," Brian said softly, staring at the photo in front of Memphis. "I don't think I would have survived those years without you to keep me sane."

"The way you complained about your high school, I'm surprised you came tonight."

"People grow up." Brian gave another vague shrug. "Things change," he said. Brian eyed him closely. "Speaking of change, are you sure I can't convince you to work with me?" he said as he took several steps closer to examine the photo of them, his limp noticeable. Memphis gripped his glass, his smile slowly fading, because he felt each uneven step as if they were flattening his lungs, making every breath sharp.

It would have been so much easier to be the one who had landed in the hospital.

"The show has a great season coming up," Brian went on. "Like I've said before, we could really use your expertise." His grin returned. "It'd be just like old times."

The words were like a punch to the gut, because Memphis longed for those days, as well. But too much had happened. Too much had changed since their reckless stunt. But if nothing else, he needed to clear the air.

"I should have called the jump," Memphis said.

Brian let a bark of laughter. "Which one of the many?"

A muscle in his jaw twitched, but Memphis pressed on. "The one that I asked you to join me for. The one that landed you in the hospital."

With a faint frown, Brian slowly turned to lean his shoulder against the wall. For a few moments he simply studied Memphis, as if adjusting to the serious tone.

And the topic of the conversation.

"The wind was too strong," Memphis said. And, for several seconds, he relived the horror of watching Brian be blown too close to the adjacent building that was undergoing construction, his chute catching on a corner of scaffolding.

The forceful slam of Brian's body against the outer wall.

His friend…hanging lifeless.

Nausea rolled, and Memphis pushed himself to go on. "I knew the wind speed was too strong and I should have called the jump." Of course, he'd been in no frame of mind to make rational decisions that day. And that had been his fault, too. He buried the disturbing memory, focusing on the here and now.

Brian narrowed his eyes, as if he didn't like the direction of the discussion. "I had been BASE jumping the same number of years as you." Brian shot him a skeptical look. "It was *my* idea to take up the sport."

"But I had more jumps under my belt."

"Dude," Brian said, a faint frown on his mouth. "This isn't a competition. And don't you dare pull the I-should-have-known-better card with me."

Frustrated, Memphis frowned. "I just—"

Brian stepped forward, his tone firm, his expression almost offended. "It was my life, Memphis. It was *my* decision. I loved what I did and I'm proud of the things I've done," he said, pausing for a moment before he went on. "And I don't want you claiming responsibility for my failures any more than I want you claiming my successes." Brian sent him a serious look and laid a hand on his thigh, the leg that had been left with a limp. "This isn't yours to own."

The seconds ticked by as Memphis fought

the need to disagree, his frown turning into a scowl along the way. Until he lost the fight and he opened his mouth to speak.

"Memphis," Brian said, cutting him off. "You know I love you, man. But you were never responsible for me. And frankly," he said, his face growing skeptical. "Your presumptuous assumption kind of pisses me off."

A surprised laugh burst from Memphis, his friend's response nothing like he'd anticipated. "Okay," he said, rubbing a hand on his neck, struggling to adjust to the unexpected turn of events. "But it wasn't my intention to piss you off."

"Good," Brian said, the moment lengthening as he eyed him warily. "Are we straight now?"

The years of guilt, the load he'd carried on his shoulders, were difficult to discard. He wasn't convinced he didn't carry his portion of blame, but sharing it with Brian made the weight easier to bear. Memphis inhaled a small breath, feeling lighter. "We're straight."

Brian hiked an eyebrow. "Does that mean you'll accept my offer to help me out with the show? It would be good to work together again."

The promising potential wound tight, competing with the rather large mountain of lingering doubts. But before he could answer, there was a stir of conversation and activity just beyond the doorway, the larger reception room now buzzing with a new energy. It took Memphis several moments to realize what the change was all about.

Dalton and his fiancée had arrived.

Leaning against the wall of the main ballroom, Brian said, "Is he a bouncer?"

"If he isn't, he should be," Memphis said, his brow crinkling in humor as he stared at the topic of discussion standing a mere twenty feet away.

Big guy. Generic suit. Eyes like a hawk. He certainly wasn't here to have fun, not with a discreetly placed radio earpiece and connecting wire that disappeared into the guy's suit.

Kate finally appeared, coming to a stop between him and her brother. "That's Dalton's right-hand man, Anthony Hall," Kate said. "The media has gathered in force, and Anthony's in contact with the security team, just in case there's trouble."

"I guarantee Anthony also researched every reunion guest who donated money to the campaign and coached Dalton on their biographical information," Brian said.

Memphis raised a brow in skeptical amusement. "You're kidding."

"It will help him work the room more effectively," Kate said, as if this were perfectly reasonable. But Memphis had his doubts.

Apparently Brian shared his concern. "Now you can see the dog-and-pony show in action, Memphis," Brian said.

"And during Dalton's schmoozing prowl of

the contributors," Memphis queried, deadpan, "will he move in order from the most important to the least? Or will the time he spends speaking with each one correlate with the amount of money donated?"

Kate shot Memphis an overly patient look. "Without contributions, Dalton can't run an effective campaign," she said easily. "And without an effective campaign, he can't get elected. One of Anthony's roles is to make Dalton look brilliant."

Her tone radiated a calm acceptance of the practice, and Memphis finally grasped just how odd her childhood had been, raised under a political spotlight. He eyed the small crowd surrounding Kate's tall, dark and high-profile ex, flanked by his redheaded fiancée. Clearly the evening was being carefully orchestrated, and the fact that the former spouses could sweep aside their differences for the greater political good was grating.

Memphis hiked a brow. "How much does one get paid to make others look brilliant?"

"Too much," Brian said, all humor gone as he stared in the direction of his former brother-in-law. "And given that Anthony's boss got engaged three months after finalizing his divorce, it appears Mr. Hall is falling down on the let's-make-Dalton-look-brilliant job."

Memphis knew Brian's hostile tone was driven by concern for his sister, but that was because her brother didn't know the full truth about her marriage.

He shot Kate a pointed look, and her eyes widened with a trace of alarm. While her brother continued to gaze unhappily at Dalton, Kate softly shook her head at Memphis, mouthing the words *not now*.

With a slight frown, Memphis opened his mouth to provide her a verbal incentive when he was interrupted by the earbud-wearing Anthony Hall, and Kate quickly traded her alarmed look for a cool social smile. But the rapid-fire blink of her eyes relayed her distress.

"Nice to see you again, Anthony," she said as the beefy blond man approached.

"Good evening, Kate," the man replied. "Dalton sent me to tell you he will be coming over to greet you now."

Brian's expression was anything but pleasant. "Why don't you use your little radio there to tell Dalton he can go to hell?"

Memphis heard a quiet "oof" from Brian, most likely in response to a discreet elbowing in the side from Kate, and Memphis decided to help his friend out.

"I don't think Representative Worthington would earn much in the way of contributions in the netherworld," Memphis drawled.

Kate's smile was weak, but her arms worked fine, giving him a matching jab in the ribs.

Anthony Hall ignored both men, addressing Kate as if they didn't exist. "We decided it would be best to give you a warning."

"Yes," Memphis murmured sardonically. "Can't be too careful with the planning."

This time Kate curled her fingers around Memphis's arm, her smile looking forced as she smoothly addressed Anthony. "Thanks for the heads-up."

Dalton's right-hand man gave Kate a polite nod and left, never having acknowledged the two men flanking her like bookends. And when Dalton himself, minus his fiancée, began to head in their direction, Kate's voice sounded strained.

"Brian," Kate said as she turned to her brother. "Why don't you go get a drink?"

Memphis could sense her growing tension.

But Brian simply scowled as his former brother-in-law drew closer. "I think I should stay."

The strain in Kate's muscles climbed to record levels.

"Please," Kate said to her brother, her heart relentless in her chest. For a full five seconds Brian continued to stare at Dalton's approaching form, clearly unhappy with her request, and Kate went on, attempting a reassuring tone. Which was far from easy. "Memphis can keep me company while I chat with Dalton."

With a reluctant expression, Brian finally blew out a breath and headed off, and Kate nearly melted with relief. But the sensation didn't last long, because when Dalton came to a stop in front of her and Memphis, all eyes in the room were aimed in their direction—or discreetly trying to pretend that they weren't.

"You're looking beautiful tonight," Dalton said

smoothly, his words sincere. "And congratulations on the reunion success." He grinned and reached out to clasp her hands. "It's another fabulous Kate event."

"Thanks," she said. She allowed her ex to kiss her cheek before discreetly pulling her palms from his, surprised by how soft they felt.

With a smile on his face, Dalton shook hands with Memphis, who calmly returned the gesture. No one would have questioned the warmth in Dalton's greeting, but Kate could see the tension framing Dalton's eyes. His handsome looks were polished to perfection, something she used to find appealing. Now she preferred a more rugged look. And calloused hands.

No need to wonder why.

"I was surprised you changed your mind about coming," she said.

"You know better than anyone that a united front benefits everybody," Dalton said, and Kate had to bite back the bitter bark of laughter. "And with that in mind," her ex went on. "I was hoping to convince you to organize an event for me."

The words were so unexpected, for a moment she couldn't process the request. She stared at her ex for several seconds before responding. "Why me?"

"Because it makes sense," he said simply, as if it did. "No one throws a better party than you. And your help will convince the public once and for all that the divorce was amicable. Besides, the Anderson name attached to anything is always an advantage," he said, his teasing smile growing bigger at the running joke they used to share.

But Kate didn't find it amusing anymore. "Have you discussed this with Olivia?"

"No," he said with a slight shrug. "Not yet."

She lifted a disbelieving brow. "Don't you think she might mind you working with your ex-wife?"

"Of course not. She knows the score."

She knows the score....

Kate blinked hard, staring at the man who had charm to spare, the one whom everybody loved. The one she'd spent years hearing about from others. How lucky she was to be his wife. How selfless Dalton was in his political goals. He hadn't discussed his plans with his future bride, confident she would approve. Because, in his mind, what benefited Dalton and his causes benefited his spouse, regardless of how she might actually feel.

Putting the needs of the many over the one. Every. Single. Time.

Mind spinning with the memories, aware every eye in the room was on her, she felt Memphis place a reassuring hand on her back, grateful for his steady presence. Just a short time ago she would have said yes to Dalton's proposal. Because she'd been trained to be a team player, to set aside her personal feelings in favor of the more important overarching goals. Her equally dedicated parents, God love them, had instilled this principle in her from the time she could walk.

And Dalton had adopted a similar attitude. But what had worked well for everyone else hadn't worked out so well for Kate Anderson.

And she was done doing what was expected.

She firmly met her ex-husband's gaze. "I won't do it."

Dalton's forehead crumpled in disbelief even as he fought to maintain a pleasant expression. "Why not?" he said. "Anthony and I think your involvement would be beneficial."

"Dalton," she said, straining for patience, but losing the battle. "You are a brilliant politician. Eloquent and convincing when you're rallying the people to address the important issues. Your concern and commitment to those less fortunate has *always* been genuine, and you are amazing when it comes to dealing with a crowd—whether it's your adoring public or your devoted staff. But when it comes to the one-on-one..." She slowly shook her head, wondering why it had taken her so long to see the truth. "You're a disaster."

The shocked look on Dalton's face was priceless. "Kate, I—"

She calmly held up her hand to stop his protest. "I'm starting my own event business," she went on, maintaining a steady gaze as she dropped her arm to her side. "And I *should* agree to your proposal and charge you *double,* just for being such an insensitive clod toward Olivia. But I'm not going to plan your event because she deserves better. Good luck with your marriage, Dalton." Heart pounding with exhilaration, she turned to leave. And then she stopped, realizing she had one more thing to say. "But this time, pay more attention to your wife."

Kate pivoted on her heel and headed for her brother, feeling lighter and lighter with every stride. Memphis fell into step beside her, his hand on her elbow.

"That was beyond awesome," he murmured. "Did it feel good?"

A smile slipped up her face. "*Better* than good."

With Memphis's touch on her arm and her ex-husband firmly in her rearview mirror, Kate felt as if she'd conquered the world, the moment a million times better than being awarded the silly prom queen title. Because this feeling was based on reality and not just an image.

Across the ballroom, her brother spied them approaching, coming to meet them halfway. "What did he want?" Brian said.

Memphis said, "Dalton asked Kate to plan an event for him."

"The son of a bitch," Brian whispered with force. And then sympathy and concern swamped his face as he looked at Kate. "Are you okay?"

Kate's heart twisted at his expression, letting out a good bit of air from her happy bubble. "Brian," she said. "It's no big deal."

"No big deal?" Her brother's face was incredulous, and a sharp sliver of unease popped the rest of her feel-good bubble. "Are you out of your mind?" he went on.

Perhaps she should have chosen her words more carefully. "I'm fine—"

"Save it, Kate," Brian said, cutting her off as he stepped closer and went on with an impatient tone. "You know he must have been seeing Olivia before your divorce." Brian's frustration was obvious, and he fixed his glare on Dalton across the room. "Why are you always so forgiving of the bastard?"

The irony actually hurt, and the sharp, barking cough from Memphis made the pain worse. Kate caught Memphis's eye and sent him a warning look, completely unprepared for this discussion. Couldn't she just bask in her recent accomplishment for a moment? *Before* she confessed the unvarnished truth to her brother?

According to the expression on Memphis's face the answer was no. While her brother continued to glare in the direction of Dalton, her heart pounded in fear, and Kate gave a slight, desperate shake of her head at Memphis, hoping to silence him. But Memphis James did what Memphis James wanted.

And now was no exception.

Memphis narrowed his eyes at Kate with heavy expectation. "Nothing wrong with a little forgiveness, Brian," Memphis said, his tone loaded. "But lies do have a way of piling up, don't they?"

Brian's gaze landed on her, and the strain on her heart grew heavy, because the combined male expressions were too much. Brian, who was worried about his sister after the mention of a supposedly cheating ex, and Memphis, who was clearly unhappy—because she was the reason her brother was needlessly concerned.

Guilt washed through her like the waters in a storm drain after a tropical downpour.

Her mouth opened to tell her brother why he didn't have to worry, but panic drove her response. "I'm okay," she said to Brian. Offering reassurance was so much easier than a confession.

"Kate," Memphis said, his tone a warning, and she knew he was expecting more from her. "You need to tell Brian the truth about the end of your marriage."

"What truth?" Brian said.

Her heart pinched so tight the drop in blood pressure made her light-headed, and she felt trapped, as thoroughly as she'd been in the bathroom. She'd lived with the lie for so long if she confessed now Brian would surely be angry she hadn't been honest with him sooner. She knew he'd been worried about her for months, but she'd been too much of a coward to set him straight.

Just like now. "The truth that I'm over Dalton, Brian," she said, gently touching his arm. "There's no reason to worry about me. I'm fine." Despite the nausea rolling in her stomach, she sent him a reassuring smile, aware of Memphis's eyes on her face, the gaze boring into her with all the intensity of a power drill. *"Really,"* she said.

As if the word was enough.

Brian let out a breath. "All right," he said reluctantly, clearly unconvinced. "You want me to fetch you a drink?"

She could use about a million of them. "Yes, please," she said, blowing out a breath of relief as Brian headed back to the bar.

Miraculously, Memphis remained silent until Brian was out of earshot.

But when he spoke, his tone weighed heavily on her heart. "If there is a repetitive stress injury for avoiding the truth, I imagine you're in a lot of pain about now."

"Memphis," she said, feeling weary.

"Why didn't you tell him the truth?"

"I want to wait until the timing is better."

"A better time?" he said skeptically, his face matching his tone. "How much better can the timing get?" The disappointment in his eyes took on a bit of anger as he pointed in the direction of Brian at the bar. "Your brother thinks you're suffering in silence and putting on a brave front."

Her stomach flipped, leaving her even more nauseated. "I know he does."

His brow developed deep furrows. "You know what I think?"

If the look on his face was any indication, she didn't want to hear.

Memphis went on anyway, the lines of anger on his forehead growing even deeper. "I think you wouldn't know the truth if it jumped up and bit you in the ass." Her heart deflated completely, and Memphis let out a small scoff. "One thing I didn't take into consideration about the possibility of moving back and working with Brian was the manual I'd need to keep up with your lies."

Despite his attitude, and the shame it brought with it, the news brought a small seed of hope. "Brian asked you to help on his show?"

"Yes."

The silence stretched between them, a soul-pounding moment where her gaze clashed with his as she waited for him to go on. He didn't. "You turned him down," she said, and Memphis didn't bother confirming the truth. She knew the answer by the look on his face.

And the remaining bits of expectation and joy from the past week collapsed in one fell swoop.

"Why won't you say yes?" she said.

He looked at her with an emotion she couldn't interpret. "Why should I?"

"Because he's your best friend," she said, her heart picking up speed. "Because you said yourself you missed working with him." It was clear from his expression that her words weren't the ones he wanted to hear. And the memories of the past week pressed hard on her chest, hope making her words tight. "And because you could continue to see me."

Several seconds passed. His expression—the doubt and the distrust and the disappointment—was hard to watch. "You've asked me several times what I want from you," Memphis said slowly, his serious tone slowly dropping the bottom on her stomach. It held an edge of finality that was frightening. "The answer used to be anything. But anything isn't enough anymore." He stared down at her, and tension gripped her muscles. "I've waited for years for you to grow up and come into your own, Kate. But maybe you were never capable of that."

Irritation flared. "That's not fair."

"You are still burying your head in the sand. If anything, it's even worse than before."

"I'm trying to fix my life."

"Not all of it. Just the parts that are easy. The hard parts are *still* being patched together with lies." The disappointment in his face was profound. "Your family doesn't know the first thing about the reality of your relationships, neither ours nor your marriage."

Heart thumping hard enough to steal her breath, aware of their surroundings, she fisted her hand, forcing herself to maintain a low voice. "My first goal was to get through this reunion. You know how hard—"

"Yes, I get it," he said. "It's *complicated*." His tone made it clear he was over that explanation. "So you are still treating me like a friend in public."

Stunned by the heat in his words, she said, "I just need more time to work through—"

"Kate," he bit out, stepping closer, the frustrated intensity in his eyes sending a chill up her back. "You keep saying it's complicated. You keep saying wait until the reunion is over. But you know what? It will *always* be complicated, and I'm finally realizing the timing will never be right enough for you." His gaze grew dark, the troubled emotions roiling in his eyes. "And I'm tired of being treated like I'm your dirty little secret."

"Dirty little—?" Confusion scrunched up her face. "What are you talking about?"

"I think you're worried your family will disown their perfect sister and daughter if they knew the truth about your past. Especially when you finally admit you cheated on your ex with a kid from the wrong side of the tracks."

The words blindsided her with a force that left her reeling, and comprehension finally forced the confusion from her tone. "Memphis," she said, losing what little patience she had left. "I'll be the first to admit I've created a big hole that I have to climb out of. But you growing up poor has *nothing* to do with any of this."

He tipped his head in disbelief. "It looks that way from where I'm standing."

Her eyebrows shot toward her hairline. "Have you even considered the possibility that your view is part of the problem? Are you that self-conscious about your roots?"

His tone was nothing but honest. "I am not ashamed of how I grew up."

"Maybe not. But you know what I think?" she said, her voice so low it shook from the effort. "I think your pride is preventing you from moving back. You're hung up about the accident because your name gets paired with a stunt gone wrong.

And the *mighty* Memphis James can't stand the way that incident tarnishes his name."

"Hell, Kate," Memphis said, his voice loaded with fury. "After making love to me, you left and went back to Dalton. Without having the decency to tell me *goodbye*. I needed to make the jump that day to burn off my anger at *you*."

Her blood leeched to her feet as the old shame, the one that had threatened to cripple her for so long, came roaring back, worse now for its role in injuring her brother. Out of confusion and fear, she'd yelled at Memphis the day of the accident, blaming him for the incident. But he'd pulled the dangerous stunt because she'd been too much of a coward to face him after what she'd done.

"I never told you, but your father showed up at my apartment two days after Brian got hurt," Memphis said. Shock rolled through her, making asking questions impossible as he went on. "Senator Anderson told me in no uncertain terms that I was a screwup and would never amount to anything."

Sorrow swamped her, and she blinked back the biting tears, trying to swallow past the horrific feelings lodged in her throat. "Memphis…"

He didn't wait for her to find the strength to respond. "I've known you for seventeen years," he went on, his voice gruff with emotion. "And I've loved you for most of them."

Anger and honesty radiated from his face as the news reverberated in her head, and Kate's heart puffed up so large she couldn't move. Until his next words came out wrapped in a prickly bitterness that held no small measure of pain. "Your father might have been the one to call me a nobody," he said, his voice hard. "But *you* are the only one who ever made me feel that way."

And with that, Memphis turned and walked out.

CHAPTER TWELVE

TEN minutes later Kate was standing in the exact same spot. Still staring at the door Memphis had exited through. Still trying to recover from his words.

Memphis loved her. Not only that, he'd loved her for a very long time. And she, in turn, had made him feel like a nobody.

Her chest burned with every breath, her throat aching from the pressure of tears that were gathering. And the agony threatened to collapse her completely. Almost ten years ago to the day she'd been at the prom with Dalton. And then several months after their graduation, he'd asked her to marry him, and she'd said yes.

It had been just one step of many in the wrong direction. Problem was, even if every step after the first had been right, she had still been led further and further astray, until she was so lost there was no hope of finding her way back.

Her life had been built on a false foundation, and the collapse had been inevitable.

Brian's voice came from behind. "Where did Memphis go?"

"He left." The hopelessness threatened to consume her. She felt like retreating to the massive hole she'd dug herself and crying her eyes out. She turned to face her brother, too defeated to accept the champagne he held in her direction. "Why didn't you tell me the reason you and Memphis did the jump the day of your accident?" Kate asked.

"What are you talking about?" Brian said, lowering the champagne flute in his hand.

She paused briefly. "That you went with Memphis because he was upset."

Brian looked surprised. "I knew something was bothering him, but he was pretty close-mouthed about what." The silence stretched, and Brian's face slowly morphed into a guarded curiosity, apparently sensing her distress. "What was he upset about?"

The fisted knot in her chest cinched tighter, and every cell in her body grew heavy. "Me."

His brow lowered in confusion. "I don't understand."

The dread grew, her heart pounding irregularly, but Kate knew it was past time to take the plunge. Because Memphis was right, she couldn't continue to avoid the issues that were growing day by day.

"I slept with Memphis," she went on.

"I'm not stupid, Kate," he said dryly. "I figured that out the morning your house looked like it had been hit by a small tornado."

She closed her eyes. Good God, suffering through the confession once was bad enough. Twice was unbearable.

"No," she said, shame piercing her before the words were even out. "I mean, before."

Brian's guarded expression returned, sharper than ever. "Before as in…?"

It was difficult to speak with such a vigorous heart rate. "As in five years ago."

Brian stared at her for several difficult seconds as his face went from total disbelief to dawning comprehension and then landed somewhere between "you've got to be kidding" and "who the hell is this woman?"

It had been difficult enough to confess. It was positively petrifying to go on.

A scowl filled Brian's face as he said, "Memphis—"

"Assumed I was free because…" Her voice faltered. "Because I asked him to make love to me."

Brian's scowl was exchanged for bug-eyed surprise, and after a moment he let out a big bark of laughter that held no humor. "Man," he said, shaking his head as he set the champagne on a nearby table. "All this time I was trying to warn Memphis away from you, telling him I'd hurt him if he broke your heart." The irony rang in his voice, and the incredulous look remained. "I was worried it was too soon for you to be getting involved."

A flush of shame spread through her gut. That was the problem with lies. One invariably needed another to be sustained, and the resulting domino effect swept you up in a wave that took on a life of its own. "Dalton and I called it quits fifteen months before the divorce was finalized."

As the uncomfortable moment stretched, squeezing her chest, Kate stared at her brother. Brian looked as if he'd just been delivered a meal he hadn't ordered, and was struggling to identify the nasty taste.

When he finally responded, he crossed his arms. "Is there anything else you'd like to share?" he said, looking at her with a large measure of distrust. "Like, you spy on foreign countries for a living?" The doubt in his face was worse than she'd imagined.

"Of course not."

"There isn't anything 'of course' about it." He shot her a cutting look and plowed his hand through his hair. "Do you know how worried I've been about you? How worried Mom and Dad have been? Right now our parents think your ex left you for another woman." He dropped his hand and went on. "Jeez, Kate. The whole freakin' town thinks the same thing." He stared at her a moment more, his expression breaking her heart. "You say it was shame, but I think you just couldn't bear to finally be the one to disappoint Mom and Dad."

Her heart lurched and a kernel of anger

popped, but she kept her voice level. "That isn't why I didn't tell them."

"Are you sure?" he said, stepping closer, his face infused with a dose of angry skepticism. "Growing up, you were bound and determined to be the ideal daughter."

"Brian," she said, exasperated by the recurring accusation that felt so unfair. "I wasn't trying to be perfect. I just figured Mom and Dad had enough trouble on their hands dealing with *you*."

His eyebrows shot toward the ceiling in disbelief.

Kate's voice grew stronger, supported by the truth. "Don't stand there and pretend you have no idea what I'm talking about. You bent over backward to be the rebel son."

"I bent over backward to be *me*."

The years of closeted resentment now freed, her words came pouring out. "All the while giving no thought to how it affected anyone else. How it affected Mom and Dad." She laid a hand on her chest. "How it affected *me*," she went on. "I used to crave one peaceful day without all the yelling. One day. Was that too much to ask?" The memories and the strain and the weariness returned, and she tried to restrain the emotion, but it was impossible to hold back now that the blunt honesty was flowing. "I swear I spent my entire childhood walking on eggshells and trying to run interference between you and Mom and Dad." Spent from her rant, fatigue settled into her muscles as the weariness consumed her, and Kate's voice fell. "It was exhausting."

Telling the truth was exhausting.

He hiked a scathing eyebrow. "So you're blaming all of your mistakes on me?"

"Absolutely not," she said firmly. Desperate to make him understand, she reached for his arm. "Brian—"

"No." Her brother held up his hands and stepped back, his expression telegraphing just how much he was over this discussion. "Sorry, Kate. I don't want to talk to you right now."

And Kate's heart crumpled completely as she watched the second most important man in her life head out the same exit as the first.

Several days later Memphis adjusted one of the specialized knee protectors beneath his jeans and waited for the crew at the end of the road to be ready. The sky was blue, the weather was warm and—despite the fact it wasn't a high fall—he was looking forward to today's gag. It had been a long time since he'd been tossed from the roof of a car. And considering the hellish roller-coaster ride of the past weeks, hitting the pavement at high speeds should be a piece of cake in comparison. At least the job came with padded clothing to help cushion his fall.

If only there was a line of gear to protect the heart, then his life would be complete.

His gaze drifted to the barricades blocking the street for the shoot. A small crowd of spectators had gathered, and he caught himself searching the crowd for Kate. Unsuccessful, he exhaled as his heart took a sharp, painful turn down bumpier roads, one of exasperation mixed with a profound ache.

It was difficult coming so close to gaining entry into heaven—near enough to knock on the door, even—only to realize he'd never be granted full access. And spending the rest of his life camped on the doorstep held little appeal.

For the umpteenth time in the past twenty minutes, his eyes drifted back to the gathering crowd, and he let out a curse, swiping his hand through his hair. Frustrated with himself. Frustrated with Kate for disappointing him at the reunion.

And frustrated that the disturbing hole her absence had created was bigger than ever. Every time Kate came back into his life and left, the part of him she took with her got bigger and bigger. But this time he owned a good bit of the blame for how things had ended.

When he'd met with Brian yesterday and learned that Kate had finally come clean about everything with her brother—and later with her *parents*—the news had both encouraged Memphis and left him uncomfortable. After twenty-four hours of deliberation he'd finally realized why dissatisfaction had been the dominant emotion.

Because what right did he have to point a blaming finger at Kate? She might have been living her life to please her parents, compelled to be the perfect daughter, but Memphis had spent the past five years intent on proving her father wrong. Memphis hadn't believed her father's claim that he'd never amount to anything, but he'd still driven himself hard to make sure the world knew that Memphis James wasn't a nobody. He'd been obsessed with making a name for himself. How pathetic.

Kate had been wrong to continue lying to her family, but she'd been unerringly right about Memphis's actions. Yet still he'd lashed out and left.

And this time you were the one who walked away.

Memphis pressed his eyes closed and, with a self-deprecating scoff, he shoved the troubling thoughts away and sucked in a slow breath.

Clearing his mind. Trying to focus.

It was a relief when the signal for the start of the stunt finally came, and Memphis climbed onto the roof of the car, a second stuntman at the wheel. Memphis hoped like hell the ride was wild enough to get Kate Anderson off his mind…at least for the next few minutes.

Kate's heart filled her mouth as Memphis clung to the roof of the car as it raced up the street, the Camaro careening wildly along the way. It was impossible to remember that the actions of the vehicle had been carefully planned in advance, and it was impossible not to come unglued as every sharp turn looked as if it would throw Memphis to the ground. Either the stuntmen were exceptionally good at appearing as if they were out of control, or they were skirting so close to the reality that it came perilously close to truth.

Kate suspected it was a bit of both.

The car took a hard turn to the left, tossing Memphis, and he sailed through the air and hit the pavement on his side, rolling for several feet before he came to a stop sprawled on his stomach. When the director called out the end of the shot, there was a round of applause from crew and spectator alike. Kate didn't join in the celebration until Memphis rolled over and leaped to his feet, as if he'd just tripped over a bump in the sidewalk and not hit the pavement at God only knows what speed. By now the crew recognized her, so slipping past the barrier was easy, until Memphis's gaze landed on hers.

His body went still, and her heart nosedived, her nerves absorbing every drop of moisture from her mouth. He looked big and he looked bold and he was so beautiful she couldn't take her eyes off him. The fact that he didn't make a move to approach her was far from encouraging, and the wariness in his expression almost made her put the moment off. But it was past time to set things right.

In truth she was running about five years and one morning-after too late.

Pushing aside the fear, she approached him on the street, ignoring the crew.

"Why are you here?" he said, his gaze wary.

Kate stopped in front of him. "To talk to you."

He stared at her for a few more seconds, every one of which was pregnant with possibility, and then he said, "I have to review the shot." Her heart crumpled a touch, but Memphis simply turned and headed for the video monitor where several men, including the driver, now huddled around the screen.

Stunned, she watched Memphis's retreating back until her brain finally recovered enough to tell her body what to do.

She hurried to catch up, falling into step beside Memphis. "I won't take long."

He didn't look at her as he kept on walking. "I need to focus, Kate."

"I want to talk to you."

He went on as if she hadn't spoken. "And if I have to do this gag again, I'd prefer you weren't around."

Heart pounding just as hard as when he'd taken his crazy fall, she pressed on. "I'm not leaving."

"Suit yourself." He came to a halt and held out his hand, stopping her in midstep. "But right now I'm going to do my job."

He pivoted on his heel, and for the second time she watched his retreating back. When he joined the six men at the monitor, she debated what to do next.

She'd known coming here would be difficult, and right now reason was telling her to be patient enough to wait until he was through. But she was tired of waiting for her life to start, and she'd learned an important lesson from Memphis along the way: if you weren't taking risks, you weren't living.

Decision made, she crossed the final ten feet. As the men watched the stunt on the screen unfold in slow motion, discussing the shot as it rolled along, Kate came to a stop behind Memphis. No one noticed her presence, the swarm of testosterone too engrossed with the scene on the monitor.

"I'll take out an ad in the paper if that's what you want," she said, her voice firm despite her skittering heart.

Six sets of male eyes turned to stare at her, everyone except for Memphis, and her discomfort climbed by several notches.

Memphis finally turned to face her, too, reluctance stamped on his expression. And since that was as good as she knew she'd get, she went on. "Because I love you, Memphis."

One of the men coughed, two looked amused and the remaining three looked at her as if she were a rabid fan gone rogue. Even Memphis appeared a touch uncomfortable.

Well…too bad.

"I'll shout it from the Anderson Tower rooftop if you want," she went on, focusing on Memphis's face lest she lose her nerve. "I'll even start an aerial advertising campaign, plastering the words in the sky if that's what it takes."

Several awkward moments passed, and Kate forced her chin to remain high despite the public scrutiny.

The driver of the car, a balding, middle-age man, broke the tension-filled silence. "I know just the pilot for the job," he said, clearly amused. "His name is George Pitka. He's the best in these parts."

"No, he ain't," another replied, obviously offended by the driver's choice. "Everyone knows that Charlie Patton is the better of the two."

A surreal moment followed as Memphis held her gaze while the two men began to seriously debate the merits of their choices, until Kate held up her hand.

"I'll keep them in mind, gentlemen," she said, sending them a strained smile. "Thanks."

Memphis took a step toward her. "I'm busy, Kate."

"You told me you loved me, Memphis. What better time is there?"

"No time like the present, I always say," the driver said, the grin of delight spreading widely across his face as he addressed Memphis. "Don't worry about us, kid. We're just starting to enjoy ourselves, aren't we, boys?"

There was a muttering of amused agreement, which only grew louder when Memphis stepped forward and took her arm, leading her away.

"You know I'll never live this down, don't you?" he said dryly.

"It builds character."

"It sabotages a guy's reputation."

"You can drive off a cliff or leap from something super tall to fix your manly name."

With a wry twist of his lips, he finally came to a stop at a quieter part of the street and hooked a hand on his hip. "Is that all you've come to do? Finally admit you love me and then proceed to humble me in front of my crewmates?" He raised a brow, waiting.

She gathered her courage. "What do I have to do to convince you to move back and give us a chance?"

The moment lingered so long Kate thought she'd squeal in frustration. Every second pounded out the impatience in her heart.

And then his mouth quirked. His tone was light, but there was a heavy thread of underlying sincerity. "I want to be wooed."

She blinked, stunned. "I don't know how," she said, her words honest. "But I *am* learning how to tell the truth."

His light tone disappeared. "That's a good start."

"I told Brian and my parents everything."

"I heard." Two more heartbeats passed. "And what happened?" he said.

"They're angry. They're incredibly disappointed in me," she said. "And I don't think they'll ever look at me the same way again." She inhaled a shaky breath, tears pricking her eyes.

His brows pulled together in a mix of tender sympathy and remembered frustration. "I've suffered a few of those moments with you myself," he said.

She sent him a small smile, blinking back the

sting of tears, knowing how much she'd hurt him in the past. "How is it possible to fall in love with a girl who made you feel like a nobody?"

His smile was soothing. "It was easy to see the potential for the woman beneath."

Easy for Memphis, the one who knew her best, but missed by the rest of the world.

"I'm taking comfort in the fact my family is now seeing the real me." Despite her efforts to keep it light, her smile faded with the memory. Facing Brian had been tough.

Facing her parents, even tougher.

"They're your family, Kate," he said in a low voice. He reached out and brushed a hair from her cheek, lingering, as if to reassure her with more than just his words. "They'll love you anyway."

Her chest grew so tight she couldn't breathe, not now that her biggest fear had been spoken out loud. "Will they?"

"They will," he said firmly. "And sometimes you have to tear down a lot in order to rebuild something better."

The pressure of tears grew stronger, and she sent him a watery smile. "I keep trying to convince myself of that." She needed him now more than she'd ever needed anyone. "Brian's finally talking to me again, albeit reluctantly. But my parents..." Her voice died as she remembered the painful confrontation, and she cleared her throat, giving a helpless shrug. She forced herself to go on, afraid of what he might say. "Will you stick around and help me through the fallout?"

His gaze dropped to his hand on her cheek, and her every cell paused as she prayed he'd say yes.

Instead of answering, he said, "A few years ago a reporter asked me how it felt to grow up poor. He wanted to know what the worst part was. I didn't have a good response then, but I've thought an awful lot about that question the past few days."

She blinked, knowing the question was vital, and dying to know the answer. "And what did you figure out?"

His thumb gently traced the corner of her mouth, his eyes on his task. "When you're raised on the wrong side of the tracks, even if you don't give a damn what other people think of you, you still belong to an invisible class. No one wants to see you."

Memphis met her gaze again, and the corner of his mouth quirked. "I already knew that part," he went on slowly. "Unfortunately, I've finally figured out it also means spending the rest of your life trying to escape..." His lips twisted wryly. "And never realizing you already have. And although all you want is for people to see you as more than where you came from, you never really trust that they do." He let out a self-deprecating laugh. "But you were right. That's my problem, not theirs."

Her heart expanded and she inhaled swiftly. "I fell in love with you that night five years ago." His gaze was steady as Kate went on. "Maybe it's horribly wrong of me," she said softly. "But I don't regret my actions anymore. I married Dalton for the wrong reasons, because he was the easier man to love, and I left him back then with no intention of going back. Making love to you that night was the first honest thing I'd done in a very long time." She sent him a small smile. "Guilt and fear drove me back, but I'm older, wiser and a whole lot braver now."

"About damn time," Memphis muttered. "I don't think I could have taken much more."

Heart soaring, she placed a hand on his chest. "So, Memphis Nathanial James, are you going to move back to Miami?"

"Actually," he said, a brow creeping higher. "This morning I called Brian to accept his offer."

Her mouth dropped open. "You little sneak," she said, lightly tapping his chest. "Why didn't you tell me?"

"I was waiting for you to come find me first."

She looked up at him, love and lightness filling every corner of her being. "Is me making a fool of myself in front of an audience enough wooing for you?"

A heart-stopping half grin crept up his lips, and he pulled her flush against him. It was hard not to melt against the hard body of the man who knew her so well. The one who had seen the best version of herself from the moment they'd met. "Angel Face," he said, his smile growing bigger, "I'd say it's a good start."

EPILOGUE

One year later

THE sand tickled her toes and the late-afternoon sun warmed her bare shoulders as Kate looked down the white shore and turquoise waters of Sunday Key, a tiny, uninhabited island located off South Beach. Streaks of purplish-pink were making their way across the sky, the beginnings of a beautiful sunset that would be the perfect backdrop for the wedding ceremony. Despite the beautiful weather, Kate knew she couldn't get *too* relaxed.

With Memphis and Brian in the same ceremony, the potential for mischief was huge.

She'd sent her brother to fetch Memphis and, as soon as she spied her soon-to-be husband coming toward her, the surge of joy was profound—no pre-wedding jitters this time around. Memphis looked handsome in his beige linen suit and white shirt, open at the throat. Kate's strapless, full length A-line gown was simple, adorned with a beige grosgrain sash that matched the color of Memphis's suit.

Waiting for the wedding to start, the thirty or so guests milled about the setting which consisted of folding chairs covered in sheer white chiffon and a bamboo arbor draped with white tulle that wound down around the poles, the fabric loose at the ends and flowing in the balmy Atlantic breeze. Simple, yet elegant, embellished only by the sunset that glowed in the sky.

Kate was certain she'd been glowing since they'd officially announced their engagement a month ago. She'd hated waiting, but Memphis had insisted on winning her parents over first.

After her confession, several weeks had passed before her parents would even talk to her again—and after that, it had taken months of cajoling to get her parents to agree to meet with Memphis. As she'd predicted, it wasn't long before her parents had grudgingly admitted he wasn't a bad guy. Her dad's softening attitude had a lot to do with how happy Memphis made her. And while the two men were too different to ever be exceptionally close, a grudging respect had developed that went both ways.

Repairing the fractured relationships hadn't been easy, but was well worth the wait.

"I thought I wasn't supposed to see my bride before the wedding," Memphis said as he sauntered closer, a gleam of appreciation in his eyes.

She bit back a smile. "You've never been worried about formalities before," she said. "Besides,

I have a question I need to ask." Kate tipped her head and looked up at him. "You don't have any surprises in store for me, do you?"

Memphis's teasing eyes grew dark. "You mean for our wedding night?"

Kate laughed. "No, I mean for the wedding ceremony."

His gaze turned secretive. "What would give you that idea?"

She playfully narrowed her eyes at him. "I spotted the pyrotechnic specialists from your stunt crew among our guests." With a raise of her eyebrow, she went on. "Am I supposed to assume their presence is a coincidence?"

His grin revealed nothing, increasing her suspicions exponentially.

"I've quizzed my brother ad nauseam," she said. "But he refuses to confess to anything."

"Brian's the best man. He owes his allegiance to me." Memphis laced his fingers with hers, pulling her close, and, despite his suspiciously evasive response, her heart turned to total mush. "If you really want to know," he said, "you should ask your dad as he walks you down the makeshift aisle."

"My *dad* is in on this?"

"Angel Face," he said, clearly entertained. "It was your father's idea."

As shock rolled through Kate, she couldn't decide whether to be happy that her father was clearly on board with her choice for a new husband…or worried that her dad was now in league with Brian and Memphis.

Given how hard she and Memphis had worked to reach this point in their relationship, Kate decided happy was the only way to be.

Her mouth twitched in humor. "I'm hoping this will be a fabulous firework display and not an over-the-top explosion."

He gave an easy shrug. "I'm not telling."

"When will I find out?" she said, smiling up at Memphis.

He tugged her closer, until she was pressed firmly against his chest—the place where she belonged. "Right after you say I do."

* * * * *

RIVA™

The full Riva collection is ready to view and buy at **www.millsandboon.co.uk/riva**, where you'll also find *Love Bites* (short films) from the team.

The Riva collection of stories is inspired by and created by women who are fun and flirty, sassy and sexy, stylish and… romantic.

Happy reading ☺

Love from Mills & Boon

Exclusive ebook

NATALIE ANDERSON
Dating & other Dangers

Some men should come with a warning sign!

Exclusive ebook

Trish WYLIE
New York's Finest Rebel

What is it that makes bad boys seem so good?

Exclusive ebook

Kimberly LANG
the Privileged and the Damned

The one man you want is the last man you can have.

www.millsandboon.co.uk/riva

RIVA/a

Exclusive ebook

Liz FIELDING
Flirting with the Italian

When a holiday fling spins deliciously out of control.

Exclusive ebook

Joss WOOD
She's so Over Him

The one that got away is back and better than ever!

MIRA LYN KELLY
Never Stay Past Midnight

He's always been the first to say goodbye...until now!

Nina HARRINGTON
my Greek Island Fling

Could every girl's dream happen to you?

www.millsandboon.co.uk/riva

RIVA/b

RIVA™

The full Riva collection is ready to view and buy at **www.millsandboon.co.uk/riva**, where you'll also find *Love Bites* (short films) from the team.

The Riva collection of stories is inspired by and created by women who are fun and flirty, sassy and sexy, stylish and… romantic.

Happy reading ☺

Love from Mills & Boon

Just another one of life's temptations…?

They sizzle on screen, they're on fire off screen.

Just a little white lie that could cause *big* trouble…

www.millsandboon.co.uk/riva

RIVA2/a

Nicola MARSH
Girl in a Vintage Dress

He could have anyone, but what he wants is the real her.

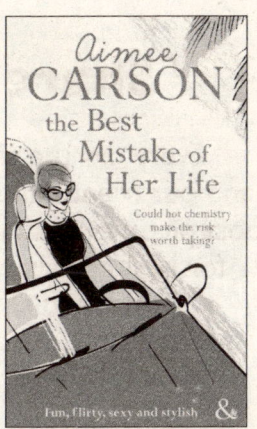

Aimee CARSON
the Best Mistake of Her Life

Does super-hot chemistry make the risk worth taking?

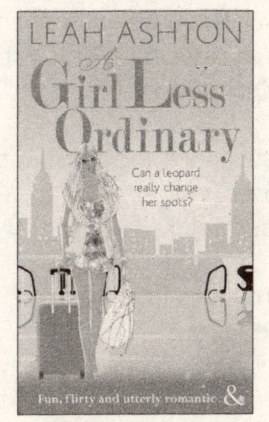

LEAH ASHTON
A Girl Less Ordinary

Can a leopard really change her spots?

Ally BLAKE
the Wedding Date

Professional suicide or best date ever?

www.millsandboon.co.uk/riva

RIVA2/b

Share the love

Every day the team at Mills & Boon—
and our friends and fans around the world—
post pictures, chat about favourite books, vote
for best covers, read free daily lunchtime
stories and share tales of romance.

Join us on Google+, YouTube and…

Sneak peeks at new covers, competitions, daily polls, free lunchtime reads, Love Bites, author news. Join us at facebook.com/romanceHQ

Riva ramblings, find your favourite authors and tweet your everyday romantic moments with #romancewatch @MillsandBoonUK

Romance-inspired destinations, food, favourite quotes and vintage cover finds at pinterest.com/MillsandBoonUK

Blogs from the team, re-blogs from writers we love, films from the team at MillsandBoonUK.tumblr.co.uk. Write a review using #Riva and you could become our next guest blogger.

www.millsandboon.co.uk

RIVA/SM